Charles Sayle

Wiclif

an historical drama

Charles Sayle

Wiclif
an historical drama

ISBN/EAN: 9783337343644

Printed in Europe, USA, Canada, Australia, Japan

Cover: Foto ©Andreas Hilbeck / pixelio.de

More available books at **www.hansebooks.com**

W I C L I F :

An Historical Drama.

Ολίγων μὲν πρακτικὸν, μεγάλων δὲ καὶ ὀνομαστῶν.

ARISTOTLE.

OXFORD:

JAMES THORNTON, HIGH STREET.

1887.

Printed by Hazell, Watson, & Viney, Ld., London and Aylesbury.

TO

THOMAS BAGOT OLDHAM,

BORN, AUGUST 18, 1861;

DIED, ASSAM, INDIA, JULY 10, 1884.

Because, when we were boys at school
  Together, and you led the way,
My three years' senior, through the rule
  Of art and science, work and play;

Because, when on a summer morn,
  Freed earlier, I had gone ahead,
Upon the boy's wheel quickly borne,
  To where our ways together led,

And swung my legs upon the gate,
  Till through the fields I saw you hie,
And when I cried to you: "How late!"
  " I bathed at Swift's," you made reply ;

(Because you loved the tiny stream,
  And knew its history more than I ;
Who treated history as a dream,
  And dreamt of archæology ;)

Because our journey that day then
  Was to the church where he had died,—
I write your name upon this when
  I lay the manuscript aside.

———

Because when on one summer morn,
  They told me *you* had "gone ahead,"—
My first dear friend, that should be torn
  Away by Death,—for you were dead ;

Because it is your turn to wait,
  For me to join you, and I see
You standing there by Heaven's gate,
  Wondering what has come to me ;

———

Because whenever Swift is named
  Your name I never can dissever
From his for whom the stream is claimed—
  Therefore your names are one for ever.

DRESDEN, APRIL 29, 1886.

*THERE are three Principles in the World,—Con-
servative, Destructive, Reformative. Each of
these is good. Each fulfils a just and right part in
the World-Soul. The Conservative preserves that
which was good pre-existing. The Destructive does
but pull down in order that the Reformative may
reconstruct and readjust. A wide survey of human
history will show that only by contemplating the
whole can we fully apprehend the true value of the
parts of which the whole is formed.*

*Those, then, err who either under-rate or over-rate
the true importance of any one of these three
Principles. Let not one exclaim that a Heretic was a
great man lest he show his littleness; nor another
extol a Preserver of Custom, lest he be proved one-
sided. Only the World-Soul can tell us, when we
have played our parts, if we have or have not served
our generation. The character of Wiclif, as por-
trayed in these pages, is an Influence, rather than a
Personality. He instilled, though he seldom did.
Wiclif stands at the commencement of the intro-*

duction of the Reformative Principle into England, whose history began for us in 1066. Not in a dissolute King but in a deep-eyed cleric, shall we find our true Prototype. In Wiclif, along with the Destructive Spirit we shall find the Reformative. Let us neither under- nor over-rate that part.

All the incidents of this play are historical. Only Janet and those scenes connected with her are the creations of the author's imagination. His main authority has been the work of Dr. Lechler, the aged Professor of Leipzig, to whom here he offers a full recognition of all his obligations.*

With Wiclif, as from a water-spring on the mountain side, began that stream of English liberty which, ever widening and widening, supports us and is our life now. With Wiclif, as its morning star, began the dawn of that fuller and freer life among us of the Reformation: and it is not yet full day.

January 1887.

---

* A translation of Dr. Lechler's work by Dr. Lorimer has been published by the Religious Tract Society.

WICLIF.

"The morning star of the Reformation."

DRAMATIS PERSONÆ.

JOHN OF GAUNT, *Duke of Lancaster.*
LORD HENRY PERCY, *Grand Marshal of England.*
SIMON SUDBURY, *Archbishop of Canterbury.*
WILLIAM COURTENAY, *Bishop of London.*
THOMAS TRILLEK, *Bishop of Rochester.*
WICLIF.
JOHN PURVEY, *Curate of Lutterworth.*
SIR HENRY CLIFFORD, *Officer to the Princess Joan.*
THE SPEAKER OF THE HOUSE OF COMMONS.
JOHN HORN, *a young priest attendant on Wiclif.*
WAT TYLER, *Leader of the Peasants' Revolt.*
JANET, *Wiclif's Niece.*
ESTHER, *her Serving Maid.*
THE PAPAL AGENT.
BACHELORS OF DIVINITY OF THE FIVE MENDICANT ORDERS.
AN OLD COUNTRYMAN.
CITIZENS OF LONDON, REVOLTERS.
MONKS, PRIESTS, PEASANTS, SOLDIERS, STROLLING MUSICIANS,
    MESSENGERS, MARKET GIRLS, ETC.

        Oxford, London, and Lutterworth.
           Time 1374-1384.

ACT I.

—

OXFORD.

—

1374.

ACT I.

SCENE I.

An English landscape in the Midlands, *shortly before sunrise.
A long pause, then the following is heard sung to slow music
from behind the stage.*

Light, light, more light
Upon the earth be streaming
    After night.
It is not good when others join the fray
    To lie dreaming.

Strength, strength, more strength
Within our veins be flowing ;
    Then at length
The life within us ever better, better
    Shall be growing.

Truth, truth, more truth,
Though some should doubt to find it ;—
    In good sooth
No easy thing ; but, found, great strength on brow
    Yet to bind it.

    [*Long pause, at the end of which the sun is seen
       to rise. When the sun has risen above the
       earth the curtain falls.*

2

Scene II.

An open space in a street in London. *Many people pass to and fro. In the foreground of the stage a group of priests. Enter a* Messenger *hurriedly.*

Cit. Steady there, fellow! Not so fast, prithee!

Mess. Had I been sent to you I would stay here,
But as it is—room! I've no time for you.

Cit. Whither's your errand, master?

Mess. Yonder, to the palace.

Cit. Well then, make way, we'll do no good to stay him.
Say, fellow, what the news?

Mess. Nay, ask not me;
Ask your own masters.

Cit. Masters? we have none.
We are no messengers.

Mess. Methinks you would not spurn to serve *my* master.

1st Cit. The Duke of Lancaster? Ay! I would serve
him.

2nd Cit. That's more than *I* would. What does he
care for us?

Cits. Nay! he is honest.

Mess. Ay! you're honest there.
It's ill praise of water if you can't drink wine.
The Duke my master is a royal Duke,
And he'll not say an evil word of me.

Enter the Duke of Lancaster, *attended by* William Courtenay, Bishop of London, *unseen to the* Messenger.

I say he loves me. Now then serve like that.

If I should wish to linger on the way,
Why! he'll not question me.
   Duke (*coming forward*).   Who told you that?
How now, you knave? Where did I send you to?
To talk to burghers in the market-place?
Haste home, you villain! I have found the Bishop,
And so outran my message. Go, I say.
[*Exit* Messenger.

(*To the* BISHOP.) So then you see the course of these
      provisions.
London but took the place of Canterbury,
And you but take the place of London now,
While Bangor comes to fill up Hereford
In order that the Pope may get thereby
The first year's fruits of every bishopric
So altered. It is a trick, I say,—a trick!
That is not all. 'Tis more than twenty years
Since the king my ~~brother~~ did enact the law
Against the nominations and provisions
Made by the Pope to enrich himself withal;
But, as you know, his priests do ever come
To feed upon us. May God's fury take them!
Think you! what news? He has not been content
To foist his grandson on us—that was bad eno';
But now he has appointed this Italian
To the Deanery of York. That brings him money,
As well as bringing to this foreign priest
His twenty thousand marks. Through all the land
Italian Cardinals and fiery Frenchmen

Do gorge upon us.   Not one place is free.
Lincoln and Salisbury, Durham and Suffolk,
And many more, are fully surfeited.
Provisions and provisions !   Why, the land
Is trodden down by all these foreign priests ;
And by this waste of gold which we can ill
Afford to have thus lost.

    Courtenay.   What says your ~~brother~~ ?

    Duke.   What says the king?   What every one must say
Who fain must do what he would fain undo.
Oh yes !   By Lady Mary, he has written
Demanding of the Pope some better course ;—
But for what use is such a vain demand ?
The Pope despises us.   The king is old.

                        [*During this conversation, the* DUKE *and the*
                         BISHOP *have been walking up and down, and*
                         the Priests *listening attentively.   The* DUKE
                         and BISHOP *go out.*

    1st Priest.   It is too much.   Too long   our land has
        suffered
From these provisions.

    2nd P.   Yet the Pope hath sent them.

    3rd P.   And therefore let us deny them.   All this
        gold
Was left for us in England,—not for them
In distant Rome.   What does the Pope with us ?—
The Pope, who earlier forced his grandson on us,
A puling youth, yet only in his teens,
And ignorant of our language.   Dignities

Which Englishmen should wear he gives away
To lisping foreigners and scheming cardinals.

2nd P.   Is not the Pope then Father of the Church?

3rd P.   But not the master therefore of the wealth
Which has been left for other purposes.

1st P.   Nay, that is true.   The wealth was meant for
　　　us,
And we will keep it.   Not but what the Pope
Is still the Church's Head.

2nd P.　　　　　　　　　Nay, that is so.

3rd P.   Therefore forsooth our master!   Patronage—
Collation—all are swallowed up by Rome;
Our king ignored, the kingdom daily weakened
By the exporting of such sums of gold
As go to feed her—her whom Christ commanded
To feed His flock, and not alone herself;
To feed His flock, and not alone to fleece it;
To strengthen all the brethren, not oppress them.
Is it not so?

1st P.　　　Yea, yea, it is too much.

3rd P.　　　Therefore, I say, let her bestir herself,
And take away this burden of provisions;
Give back the patrons all the patrons' rights;
And give us all the right of free election,
Ceasing from injury to the kingdom's rights.
Perchance, if she do this,—perchance, I say,—
The land's devotion may revive for her.

2nd P.   It is most certain that we are her subjects.

1st P.   Subjects, yea! in matters of the faith,

But not in bullion—there the buskin galls.

2nd P.　You heard the King has written to the Pope
Demanding his attention for the matter?

3rd P.　Yea, yea! I know; and yet his agents come.
See, there is one of them!

> [*An* Agent *clad in the Papal livery passes. The
> people groan at him under their breath. As
> he passes the* Priests, *the* Third Priest *mutters
> at him.*

3rd P.　　　　　　　　　　God's curse on you!
Agent.　How said you?
3rd P.　　　　　　　　　　Better not to ask again,
Unless you would be burdened with a curse.

> [*The* People *assemble themselves round.*

Agent.　Do you know this livery?
3rd P.　　　　　　　　　　　Too well.
The People.　　　　　　　　　　Too well,
A damned Pope's agent.
Agent.　　　　　　You shall hear of this.
One of the People.　Ay, that we will, and you perhaps
　　shall feel it. (*Striking him.*)
2nd P.　'Twere better, sire, to stay no longer here,
The crowd's uneasy.
Agent.　　　　　　Rabble! untaught curs!
People.　Ha! ha! Have at you, drainers of our soil!
Now, "untaught," rabble did you hear the words?
Set on him!

> [*The crowd set on him. He escapes with difficulty,
> the crowd following.*

3rd P.   Did you mark that incident ?
The people are for us,—so then our cause will win,
So give us time and men to guide our way.

   2nd P.   Too few, too few.

   1st P.   Yet one were even enough.

   3rd P.   Then pray to heaven we may find the man.
Too long our land has suffered.   It is time.

SCENE III.

WICLIF'S *garden at* Oxford *in Canterbury Hall.   To the right the
   Wardenage, to the left a wicket gate opening into the street
   through a low wall.   Morning.   Summer-time.* JANET *dis-
   covered playing at ball with her two maids.*

Janet.   Throw it to me, Esther, throw it to me !
Ha, ha ! you nurse !   Now then, again, again !
There in the bushes.   Now, nurse, catch this time !
Take care ! the garden is small.   It will go over.

> [*The ball goes over the wall.*

Ah, now it is lost !   Quick through the wicket gate !

> [*She runs to the gate.   As she reaches it, the gate
> opens and enter* JOHN HORN *with the ball.*

John.   Lady, this ball is yours.   Is it not so ?
It fell down at my feet on entering.
I come to seek the Warden.   Forgive me if
I tumbled in upon your privacy.

Janet.   I thank you !   We were playing boisterously,
Too much so.

   John.   I was honoured in your fault.
The ball fell at my feet, I brought it you.

Janet. You seek my uncle?

John. If he should be within.

Janet. He is within. Shall I summon him for you?

John. Nay, nay! Your game's disturbed.

Janet. My punishment
For too high-reaching throws.

Enter WICLIF.

Ah! here he comes!
Uncle! here is a pupil that has asked for you.

Wic. What does he here?—Ah, you, friend John, 'tis
you.
Is he a graduate in your playing here?

Janet. Nay, but he brought our wool-ball, which had
fallen
Beyond the wall.

Wic. Ay well, love, leave us now.

Janet (*kissing him*). My noble uncle.

[JANET *goes out.*

Wic. Now, friend John, with you.

John. Master, you have been very changed of late.
They say within the city you are changed.
They talk of rising storms and coming wars ;
And when they talk they ever talk of you.
They say you hate the Pope who is our master,
And would take arms against the Church's cause.
Have I heard right? What must I hear of this?

Wic. Do they talk so? Then let them talk awhile.
I have my work, which none but I can do.

Whether it lead so far as they do say,
Time's self alone can tell you.   Answered so ?

John.   Nay, master, you make fear weak.   I pray you
    more.
We look to see you Cardinal one day ;—
How should you be it, fighting with the Pope ?

Wic.   I will not fight.   I will have reverence
And order in my task, not blind affray.
Whoever strikes, it shall not first be I.

John.   Why, master ! must I dub you heretic ?

Wic.   Take you the word, John, I must do with deeds.
And if they be heretical, I die ;
If they be not, I live.   The cast is there.

John.   Are these thoughts thus ?   But, master, bear with
    me,
I came to ask you for a sacred task—
If you should leave us and go hence to fight,
Take me then with you.   I will serve you then.

Wic.   Nay, nay, boy, nay !   I will go forth alone.
But wherefore do you speak so wretchedly ?
I am here, your Warden.   Yonder is the Pope.

John.   Ay, but they say there'll be no stopping here,—
That you will leave us.

Wic.   Say they so, indeed ?
Ah well ! I shall not stay.

John.   And must I stay ?
Methinks that I could spend my life with you
In rendering service to your every want,
Whether you go or stay.

Wic. Boy, boy, you rave.

John. I do not rave indeed.

Wic. Well, we shall see.

John. But you will yet be made a Cardinal.
Promise me that. Then will I serve you too.

Wic. Peace, peace, boy! You jest with words.

John. But how shall I answer those that speak you
thus?

Wic. Say that the Pope will make him Cardinal
Who will be Cardinal when he is made;
And as for me, I am as other men
Whom God has made for living. Prithee leave me now.

John. I have tired you, master.

Wic. Nay! I would be alone.

John. Then I must leave you.

[*Kissing his hand.*

So, my honoured father.

[*Exit* JOHN.

Wic. So then they speak of me. The die is cast.
Backwards or forwards,—there's no resting here.
A Cardinal is what these poor half souls
Would have me be,—a Roman Cardinal.
No, no! It is not good, it is not good.—
So must it be then,—sacrifice or nought,
When all is so uncertain. Sacrifice
Was always good, from Abel's until now.
And all the great men of the buried past
Beckon towards me. Yes! the cause is great,
And what I lose is less than I shall gain.

Base thought! God grant me better in my heart,
God grant me better in the days to come,
Than thus to think of red-robed Cardinals,
When I would seek the Truth, and follow Christ—
As I will follow.   Yes! the cause is great.
So great extortion·over all the land
That cries against the oppressors.   O Lord Christ!
To look at Christendom as she is now,
How must it seem that Thou hast never died.
But that Thou hast, we know it.   Therefore now
Be Thine the model which our life should choose,
Even up to Calvary, if so it must.

[Looking up into the sky.

Methinks there are no clouds now in the sky;
Would it were so in England!   Where's the wind
To drive them from us ere we die of cold?
The king is good, but he grows old through years;
The nobles are too weak and too divided;
Our prelates too obsequious to our foe.
There is not one.   It is too long to wait
Till little Richard mounts his father's throne,—
The throne, alas! his father never filled.
The game is hazardous when a young king reigns.
So must we wait until the moment comes.—

A Messenger comes in.

How now?
   Mess.   I seek the Warden.
   Wic.   I am he.
   Mess.   Then are these letters yours.

Wic.   I thank you, sir.
Seek some refreshment in the house within.

> [*The* Messenger *bows.*

Whence come you ?
    Mess.   From the city.
    Wic.   That is well.

> [*He signs to him to retire, then opens the letters.*
> *He reads.*

" *The excitement still grows.   Yesterday in the city
the Papal agent while passing through an open square
was set upon by the mob, and barely escaped with his life.
Fresh exactions are heard of every day.   The barons,
knights, and burgesses have written to the Pope, demanding alleviation.   We must stand together.*"

Ay, and so we will.   The time is ripe,
And all the country cries aloud for vengeance.

> *Enter another* Messenger *in the* DUKE OF LANCASTER'S *livery.*

I see from whence you come, and therefore now
I give you greeting.   Is your master well ?
    Mess.   My master sends you greeting by my mouth,
And bids you not forget his cognisance,
Nor how you spent the time you were at Bruges,
As the Duke's companion on the embassy ;
And bade me to deliver these to you.
    Wic.   I thank you : seek refreshment in the house.

> [*Opening the letter.*

It should be something good, the cover tells me.

[He reads.

" The King has need of one who knows the law and
hates the Pope. I have mentioned you to him, and
advised him to ask the Chancellor to make a choice
of such a man and send him. Therefore it is for you to
see the Chancellor and gain your appointment. Now is
the time to strike. Therefore delay not. Remember me,
and the days we spent at Bruges."

A kingly letter, and a politician's.
No, I will stir not.   Others here shall seek me,
If I am worthy for their services ;
Else were a better worsted.

Ho, there within,

A Serving Maid appears.

Pray send to me the messenger that came
From the Duke of Lancaster.

[She goes in.

There's need to send

Some answer.

Enter the DUKE'S Messenger.

Prithee, do you return to-night ?

 Mess.   That rests with you : I wait upon your service.

 Wic.   Then find some decent lodging in the city,
And let the host provide you what you want.
The hostels here are good.

 Mess.   I thank you, sir.

[He goes out.

Another Messenger *comes in.*

Mess. I come from the Chancellor with these for you,
With which he sends his congratulations
Upon the honours that are named therein.

> [*Giving him a letter. He opens the letter in haste,*
> *and reads it.*

" *The King has written us to send a goodly man, that*
knows the King's cause and the sins of Rome, to be his
cleric in the Parliament, and we together have just deter-
mined here on sending you. Therefore, God speed, for
you have much to do, and haste to do it. In that you are
Warden of Canterbury Hall, we ourselves will see that
this is well administered."

(*Aside.*) So has it come at last. My lot has fallen.
Now, Wiclif, go to prove what you would prove,
And heal a nation by a nation's love.
Return now answer to the Chancellor,

> [*To the* Messenger.

That I do thank him with a grateful heart,
And tell him that I will not fail to act
The part which suits me. Take my greeting back.

> [*The* Messenger *goes out.*

Now, Wiclif, hast thou need of all thy strength :—
God grant me strength to conquer.

> [*He goes out.*

Scene IV.

The open road, on a high hill, leading from Oxford *to* London. *The towers of the city of* Oxford *are seen in the distance.* WICLIF'S *cortège is coming up the hill,* WICLIF *walking behind.* Servants *talking.*

1st Servant.   How many miles from Oxford have we come ?

2nd Servant.   A barely seven ; we have far to go.
See, there the city lies down in the mist.

1st Ser.   Plagues on all travellers at this time of day.
I shall not see my Kit now many a week.

2nd Ser.   Ay ! 'tis poor service : yet when masters call
We must obey them, since they are our masters.

1st Ser.   What do they want with him in Parliament ?

2nd Ser.   Have you not heard, the king has sent for him ?

1st Ser.   Ay ! and the King doth send for criminals.
It is not so, I hope, the King hath sent.

2nd Ser.   Now, by St. Thomas, what a loon you are !
It is an honour which he has conferred.
You should be glad when so our Master rises.

1st Ser.   I wish his rising was not up this hill,
'Tis weary work on such a day as this.

2nd Ser.   Do you see Abingdon away there, right ?
Its spire looks pretty with the light upon it.

1st Ser.   Ay ! and I see a horseman coming to us.
I wish I had his horse and he my duty.

2nd Ser.   He is well-clad and rides a goodly steed.
Is that some livery that he has on ?

1st Ser. It seems so, or he would not ride so fast.
We are more careful when the goods are ours.

2nd Ser. 'Mary! he comes towards us. We shall see.
The livery he wears is like the King's.

1st Ser. No; the Archbishop's! Any fool knows that.

2nd Ser. You were a fool, then, not so long ago.

> [*They pause. A mounted* Horseman *enters. Meeting them, he pulls up.*

Horseman. Has Master Wiclif left the city yet?

2nd Ser. He is behind us. 'Tis his company.

Hor. Ah! That is lucky. I have news for him.

Wic. (*coming forward*). What would you, friend?

Hor. You may not call me "friend"
When you have read these letters that I bring.

> [*Giving him letters.*

I come from the Archbishop.

Wic. He is well?

Hor. Indeed, too well it fain would seem for you.

> [WICLIF *reads the letters. He is much moved.
> He turns round and gazes on* Oxford. *A
> long pause.*

Wic. Most things I could have borne, but hardly this.

> [*He pauses again. Then addressing his followers.*

My friends, it seems my presence is displeasing
To this man's master in the Wardenage.
The new archbishop, to his office raised,
And finding that our monks were secular
As well as all our scholars, has deposed
Myself from being Warden of the Hall,

Thereby reversing all its Founder's wishes,
Who placed me, as you know, to be its head.

Ser.   My Master, O my Master, curse the day!

Wic.   Myself I do not care; but it doth seem
He has appointed to his place anew
The ancient Warden who had been deposed.

Ser.   What! Warden Woodhall and his bacchanals?
O Master, Master! What will you now do,
Being thus thrown out?

Wic.   Do? As an honest man
I do accept what 'tis not mine to alter.
But that my cup is not all filled with gall,
He does inform me that the King hath raised
This same John Wiclif to the Rectorate
Of Lutterworth upon the river Swift,
Within the diocese of Lincoln.   So
I am not left quite homeless.

Ser.   Ah! we know
The King's our friend, whatever prelates do.

Wic.   Lead on, I beg you; this makes no delay.
We must be far upon our road to-night.

> [*The* Servants *go out leading. The* Horseman *remains.*

Wic.   And you, sir, follow in our train as well.
Those who do bear ill news must not be made
To bear the consequence of evil moods.
You shall be cared for.   Lead! I walk straight after.

> [*The* Horseman *turns his horse and follows.*
> WICLIF *is left standing alone. He pauses for*
> *a long time, looking at* Oxford. *At last he*
> *speaks.*

3

Wic.   Sink down into the mist, ye long-loved towers!
It is not yours to feel the life that throbs
About your feet.   This from you Nature robs,
Lest you should wake to feel this life of ours.
Sink down!   We can but feel your mystic powers
Engender in our hearts deep swelling tears,
Seeing we shall not see what light enrobes
Your beauty through the length of many years.
Oh!   There's a spirit in your silent stones
That breathes in us a passion we do feel
Pulsing within us,—how, we dare not tell.
And little now for this lost love atones
Of our kind mother from whose side we steal,—
The Oxford we have loved and loved too well.

[*He goes out, following the cortège.   The curtain falls.*

ACT II.

——

PARLIAMENT.

——

1376.

ACT II.

SCENE I.

A street in London. *Many people. Enter* WICLIF. *On the opposite side of the stage enter a* Servant *wearing the livery of the* DUKE OF LANCASTER.

Ser. Are you not Master Wiclif?

Wic.   The same is he.

Ser. Then am I sent to find you by my master,
Even the noble Duke of Lancaster,
Who bids you seek him when you earliest can
Within his palace in the Savoy.

Wic.   I will.
Is the Duke at leisure?

Ser.   So I do believe.

Wic. Then bear him word that I will seek him soon,
And if he wish, will see him presently.

Ser. I will.

Wic. Lead on, and I will follow straight.
                                        [*They go out.*

SCENE II.

A room in the DUKE OF LANCASTER'S *Palace in the Savoy.*
The DUKE *alone.*

The Duke. So all my plans shall prosper, and myself
Shall be omnipotent,—no trivial thing,

And therefore to be aimed at. The old King
Is fast approaching to his latter end ;
Edward is dead who should have been our king,
My elder brother ;—elder brothers die
Conveniently sometimes ;—and Lionél—
He, too, is dead, and I alone am left.
But Edward left a child—God's curse on him !—
Who will not die ; and he will be our king—
King Richard—unless indeed King John
Should chance to slip into the throne before,
The kingdom's better keeper. But a child,
E'en though he grow to be a stalwart youth,
Shall hardly rule the kingdom as one would
Who has been ruling all through many years,
A king without the name. Why, then, the name
Must follow, and I needs must strive
To make it do so. Therefore am I here
Contriving how such end may follow on
Most fitly and obediently to nature.
Further, I see, the land is sadly ruled
By prelates and priest-puppets and the like ;
This should not be, and would not were I king.
But now they hate me, and had nigh ruined me
When I sprang up and turned the tables on them.
Much luck they won them ; he of Winchester,
William of Wykeham, being banished from the court,
As every bishop should be. I have stopped
The Commons' Speaker, Peter de la Mere,
With lodging in a prison—that's for comfort.

Now then the matter is to learn to stay
The Papal power and nurse our revenues;
For those who reign must have wherewith to reign.
This will I do.—The time grows on apace.
I had expected Wiclif ere this hour.
Methinks that I can use him for myself,
For am not I the State that is to be,
And the State but I myself?

Enter a Servant.

Ser.   May it please your Grace,
The reverend Doctor Master Wiclif waits
Upon your bidding.
 Duke.   Bring him here to me.

          [*Exit* Servant.

Now shall I know what further I may hope
From this man's service.   Much I fully hope,
But sadly fear me lest his faith should fail.

Enter the Servant, *followed by* WICLIF.   WICLIF *makes a
deep obeisance.*

 Ser.   May it please your Grace, he is before you.
 The Duke (signing towards him).   Leave us.

          [*Exit* Servant.

(*To* WICLIF.)   It is some years since last we met at
   Bruges.
You are much altered since that time, I think.
 Wic.   Indeed, I have done much.
 Duke.   And nobly too,

If I may judge from all things that I hear.
Is it not so?

    Wic.   That must others judge, not I.

    Duke. Most nobly answered. You are here to-day,
Being summoned by the King to Parliament.
Thus much you know, but know not that 'twas I
That urged the King to fetch you.

    Wic.   I thank your Grace;
If 1 can serve—

    Duke   Nay, that I know already.
You wear the people's cause most well at heart,
And therefore mine.

    Wic.   If yours should be the people's.

    Duke. Ay, that it is, as you yourself should know.

                         [*He pauses.*

I sent for you on certain matters of State,
That now are weighty, and will soon be public.
You know—and, did you not, you soon would know—
Of certain coalitions which were made
Against my influence within the realm.
How I do stand regarding matters of church
My fall, as then accomplished, will inform you.
But now, praise Holy Mary! once again
I rise to my old station in the State.
The Speaker of the Commons is imprisoned;
She who is called the Queen is summoned back;
And of the prelates, William of Winchester
Is banished from the court, with loss besides
Of the temporalities of his own see;

Lords Latimer and Percy are recalled,
So is our star ascendant once again.
Now travel further ;—for as much as this
You know, or may have known, I say, already ;—
It is not long since we did hear the news
Of princely Edward's death, the heir apparent,
Wherein the nation lost a goodly king.
You follow me ?

Wic.   I do, my liege.

Duke.   Well then,
As his successor, is there none to follow,
In line direct, except this infant boy,
Young Richard, his own son,—you follow me ?

Wic. I do.

Duke.   The State has need of councillors
Who care for it and guard it till this boy
May grow perchance to fill his grandsire's throne.
This grandsire, being too weak to have long to live,
It were as well to see to things of State,
Lest they be mangled, wasted, trampled on,
Through lack of guidance.   You do catch me now ?

Wic. Your Grace ! it is yourself you mean should take
The helm in case of danger—am I right ?—
Till Richard is of years.

Duke.   Till it may seem
That he is fit to govern by himself.

Wic. Your Grace, I go with you.

Duke.   Therefore it seems—
For that the King is old, yea, passing old—

We must now husband all the nation's strength
To grasp with danger.   Dangers are there many
From France, from Rome, from Scotland, and from Ireland ;
I haste to ask if you will work for me
In matters of the Church and of the State ?

Wic.   I read, your Grace, your thoughts imperfectly,
But here I render answer as I may,
That in all good and in all fair emprise
Will I accompany your Grace's path ;
For ever do I lend what weight I have
To those who govern orderly and well.
Moreover, in past years I saw, I think,
That we had much, ay, many, things in common.
In these, then, am I with you.   Yet in all,
Whether I be or not at one with you,
That time alone can prove.   You have my answer.

Duke.   I thank you.   When it seems that I do go
Too far upon this path then may you speak.
But so far am I with you thoroughly—
Against the Pope, against the prelates too—

Wic.   (*interrupting him*).   In matters of the State.

Duke.   Ay ! of the State :
You have no need to ask.   The rest is nought.

Wic.   The rest is more than nought.   The rest is some-
        thing
That doth demand obedience in the State.

Duke.   Ay, ay! that may be.   In affairs of State
I think we are together.   Is it not so ?

Wic.   Your Grace, I have three duties to perform

Which I dare not omit.　The first I call
My duty to the Truth, which is the greatest.
The second is as great,—or nearly so,—
My duty unto Christ, our Saviour.
These two let each man keep for ever by him.
But third is that same duty which I have
Unto myself, a duty which is harder
Than the other two.　This dare I not evade,
Seeing therein doth gather everything.
Methinks that I again have answered you.

Duke.　A somewhat riddling answer.　Yet I take it.
On Monday is convened the Parliament—
You will be there?

Wic.　　　　　　'Tis therefore I am here.

Duke.　I wish you luck; there is much work to do.

Wic.　There is, my liege.　Have I your leave the while
To take my leave?

Duke　　　　You have.

Wic.　　　　　　　　I thank you for it.

　　　　　　　　　　　　[*He goes out.*

Duke.　Unruly, yet still useful—as are all.

　　　　　　　　　　　　[*The curtain falls.*

Scene III.

A room in the ARCHBISHOP'S *Palace at* Lambeth.　*The* ARCHBISHOP
and the BISHOP OF LONDON.

Bishop.　So great the Duke of Lancaster does grow
There will be no restraining him ere long,
And he is hostile now more than before,

When we half conquered and sent off the Queen.
Therefore I know something must be devised
Against his greatness.

    Arch.   You speak bitter truth.

    Bishop.   Bitter as wormwood.   Yet is this not worst,
For he hath taken up in his protection
. This heretic, John Wiclif, whom the King
Has sent for ; and he fights against the Pope,
Our lawful head.   Something must we now do
That shall be capital against the Duke.
The Duke hath ruined us ; it is our turn—

    Arch.   To ruin now the Duke.   The Prelates' task !

    Bishop.   The Prelates who held office in the State
Have been removed by his sole agency
Saying that laymen alone must rule the realm.

    Arch.   His tenure now of Canterbury Hall
Was on this head; but now our plans prevail.
He has been ousted now from this position.

    Bishop.   You speak of trifles when the realm's at stake,
As one that in a war retires himself,
And sets about composing melodies.
Let news be sent of Wiclif's words to Rome ;
So will we kill the jackal and the lion
Both with one stroke.

                Enter BISHOP OF ROCHESTER.

                    All hail, now, brother Prelate !

    Bishop of Rochester.   And I, too, greet you; take my
        greeting both.

    Arch.   We counsel of the Duke of Lancaster,

Who has attacked our powers.   It is now time
To answer blow by blow.   It seems that he
Is much beholden to this John of Wiclif,
Whom must we now attack as heretic,
Being indeed what we would have him be.
Therefore we think it wise to apprise the Pope
Of his performance.

   Rochester.   Indeed, the step is good.

   Arch.   Then shall it be performed this very day.

   London.   That were well fixed on. He has talked enough,
And it is time to stop his eloquence.
Yet,—for a mighty fire is first a flame,
As tiny as a pin's head, among the tinder.
And so a small beginning leads to ruin,
Which, stopped in time, had saved the whole unburnt,—
Do I besides propose that we should take
The matter in our hands.   The Convocation
Would sure approve our action in the case.
I say we must not let this flame increase,
As it might do if left to its own course.
Till messengers can go and come from Rome,
Were it not best to cite the man as well
To appear before us in our proper court ?

   Arch.   That is a weighty matter.   We have need
To think upon it.   Mighty is the Duke.

   London.   And we are mightier.   In our veins, as his,
Flows royal blood.   Yea ! and our life is nobler
Who seek to stay and not pull down the realm.
Is traitor's blood still royal ?

Roch.   .   This I know,
Such action would delight the agèd King.
Who can love to see men barter for
The crown which he yet holds a little while !

   London.   It would be politic,—this traitor thrown,
And in the throw the heretic as well
Silenced.

   Arch.   Ay ! heretics must be suppressed.

   London. Do you suppress, then, this one. 'Tis your place.

   Arch.   Indeed, it seems so, and you argue well.
I will see to it.   Lend we help awhile,
And Convocation shall approve the act.
There will be time before the Parliament.

   London.   That is well said.   We must not now delay.

   Arch.   You do approve it, brother of Rochester ?

   Roch.   I, your Grace ?   Yes, I approve the act.

   Arch.   Then come with us.   We may have need of State.

   London.   We must not linger, for the Parliament
Doth meet at noon, and somewhat earlier
The Convocation has been called together.
If this must pass beneath their proper seal
Then must we hasten.

(*To* Rochester.)   Do you go with us ?

   Roch.   I have some need of leisure.   I remain.

   London.   As you do wish.   Your zeal doth not lie in it.

               [*The* Archbishop *and* Bishop of London *go
                 out.* Rochester *left standing.*

   Roch.   William of London, I do hate your visage.
A bishop and no bishop in one form,

A bishop and a noble of the realm,
Within whose veins the blood of Edward flows
Too strongly and too fully.   Woe the day
When on your shoulders higher mantles fall,
If thus you plan a poor priest's overthrow
For plans of State !   A saintly bishop, you !

[He goes out.

SCENE IV.

A corridor in the House of Parliament.   The ARCHBISHOP OF
   CANTERBURY *and the* BISHOP OF LONDON *conversing.*

Arch.   Are you content with these same steps we take ?

London.   I am, your Grace ; yourself shall see them
      good.

Arch.   I do not doubt it.   Heretics must cease.
Yet do I fear the King may like it not,
That we should thus attack whom he has chosen
To hold his case upon these revenues.

London.   If he did know, as he shall fully know,
Why we have done it, he will take our part.
Moreover, he has fully now rewarded
This Wiclif with the living which he gave him
At Lutterworth.

Arch.   Is it not time to go
And hear the question in the House discussed ?

London.   It is, and we will enter.   Mark you now
He will receive the summons we have written
While he is speaking.

Arch.   Let us go within.

[They go out.   The middle curtain rises.

SCENE V.

The House of Commons. WICLIF *present.* *The* BISHOP OF ROCHESTER *standing by listening, the* SPEAKER *in the chair. The* ARCHBISHOP OF CANTERBURY *and* BISHOP OF LONDON *also listening.*

Speaker. Upon this matter of the subsidies
There must be some course taken that will meet
The debt.　I bid you take it honestly.
If any wish to speak so let him speak,
Or else for ever after hold his peace.
You, Master Wiclif, have you nought to say
That is pertaining to these subsidies ?

Wic. I thank you, my Lord Speaker, for your call,
For I have much to say, and wish to say it.
Therefore I bid you hear me patiently,
Seeing I speak for all the country's good.
First, then, all now here present are advised
By whose command I stand before you all,
Being summoned by the King, our Lord and Master.—
Therefore I bid you listen patiently.
But that I have another One's command
Ye also know, whose summons I obey
More and not less than his—my Master Christ's.—
Therefore I bid you listen patiently.
And that I follow Christ no less than him,
The King our Master, this I strive to show.
—You say the realm is poor.　How comes it then
That every year such moneys leave the realm
As are five times as great as those the King

Receives in taxes ?   Yea, how comes it then
That all the first-fruits leave the country so ?
Thus much I know, and many ills besides ;
But these, the chief, I mention.   Need I add
That yet another twenty-thousand-marks
Is sent to all the absent cardinals
Each several year?   The vacant bishoprics
The Pope with stale-grown priests replenishes,
And his own purse with the first-fruits of each.—
Yet do you wonder that the realm is poor ?

> *A Member.*   These things are owed the Pope, who
> is our head.

Wic.   But not our Bursar or our Judas-brother,
As this one would become.   Yes, yes ! I know
What he and his would say.   But I reply,
And here remaining am prepared to prove,
That all his claims are long since forfeited.
It is ten years since he last challenged us,
And we replied he had no claim on us,
Being ready to fight thereon.   Therefore I say
These moneys that are issuing from the realm
Are wrongly squandered, and the flock of Christ
Is thereby fleeced and shorn, not fed and nurtured.
So would I answer you upon this matter.
I thank you that you heard me patiently.

> [*The* ARCHBISHOP *and* BISHOP OF LONDON *go
> out quickly.*

1st Mem.   Indeed he argues justly.
2nd Mem.   Ay, that's so.

4

3rd Mem.　We should do well indeed.

Speaker.　　　　　　　　　　　　Does any speak ?

Roch. (*pulls* WICLIF *by the arm*).　Are you mad,
　　Wiclif ?　Are you wholly mad ?
Do you know the Pope's already cited you,
And speak you thus ?　The thing is almost death,—
Indeed, worse has been suffered.

Wic.　　　　　　　　　　　Sir, again
I turn to address you.　Some may-be there are
Who hold themselves subservient to the Pope,
As I do, as the head of all the Church,
By Christ appointed.　Some besides there are
Who hold him, too, the head of all the realm,
But so not I.　Therefore if any wish,
And if they have that they would wish to say,
So let them.　Here may every burgher speak.

Bishop (*in his ear*).　I caution you there are bad minds
　　at work ;
Desist in time.

Wic. (*answering him*).　I know not to desist,
Take back that answer, an it please your Grace.

Bishop.　Well, well ! you are determined.

Wic.　　　　　　　　　　　You speak truth.

Speaker.　I ask you, gentlemen, assembled here,
If we should send some such memorial
Up to the King that he may know thereof ?

Members.　Ay, verily.

Speaker.　　　　　　Then shall the thing be done.

　　　　　　Enter a Messenger.

Mess.   A message for the Reverend Master Wiclif.

Wic.   Give it me here.

> [*The* Messenger *hands him a letter.   He tears it open and reads.*

(*Aside.*)   Ha! signed by an unknown name.

I love not such.   Now let me read again.

> [*He reads.*

" *You must beware of the Duke of Lancaster.   He only seeks to use you as his weapon, which he will throw away when done with.   Therefore be warned in time.   Moreover, the Bishops' party seek to ruin you that he may be entangled therein.   Therefore doubly avoid him.   I say this for your good.*—ONE WHO WISHES FOR YOUR WELFARE."

(*Aside.*)   So.   Is the eagle false?   Yet not false I.

I have my task, which I would fain complete,

Whether the Duke be willing or will not;

As for the Bishops—I must follow Christ,

Whatever Popes and Prelates choose to do.

Bishop.   You are moved, Wiclif?

Wic.   No, your Grace, not much,

Only some news that reaches me from home.

Bishop (*aside*).   I had thought it different.   (*Aloud*)
      That 'tis no more I'm glad.

> [*Aside, as the door opens and the* ARCHBISHOP'S Messenger *comes in.*

Ah! here he his.

Mess. (*to Wiclif*).   This, sir, is meant for you.

> [*He hands him a paper.*

Wic. (*reading\it and then returning it*).   I pray you
　　read it here aloud.   Perhaps
There may be some who know it not as yet.

[*He looks at the* BISHOP.

(*To the* SPEAKER.)   I crave your leave.
　Speaker.　　　　　　　　You have it.
　Wic.　　　　　　　　　Take my thanks.

Mess.   " *To John Wiclif, Professor of Sacred Theology
in our University of Oxford, these :—You are hereby cited
to appear before your spiritual judges on the* 19*th of
February next approaching, in the Lady Chapel of our
Cathedral of·St. Paul's in the city of London, to answer
certain charges of heretical doctrine which you are supposed
to hold.   You shall absent yourself therefrom on peril.
The Lord have mercy on your soul, as on all heretics.*"

[*There is much commotion.   The* Members *gather
round* WICLIF.

　Wic.   I am not wont to run away from danger,
Nor shall I now.
　The Members.　　　Nay, indeed, we will protect you.
　Wic.   I thank you, sirs, but I shall need you not,
For either your protection would serve not,
Being a point of Church-established usage,
Or else these men are liars who write so.
Nay, nay, indeed I fear not.
　The Mem.　　　　　Do not fear.
　Wic.   That shall I not, for I go forth among them
To guard God's Truth, whoever else may lie.

[*The curtain falls.*

ACT III.

HIERARCHY.

1377-81.

ACT III.

SCENE I.

A Street in London. *Early morning.* Workmen, Citizens, *etc.,*
going to and fro. A distant clock strikes five.

1st Cit.   God's greeting, citizens; how is't with you?

2nd Cit.   I thank you, citizen, the ship's afloat.

1st Cit.   What is the hour?

2nd Cit.   A trifle after five.
Did you not hear the hour strike at St. Paul's?

1st Cit.   By the blessed Mary I did not.   I must hasten.

2nd Cit.   Well, prosper work then!   Do you go to-day
To the Cathedral to listen to the trial?

1st Cit.   I do not know.   It may be.

                                        [*He goes out.*

A Workman (*to* 2nd Citizen, *seizing him by the arm*).
      Come along, sir.
They say the church is filling up already,
There'll be no room to see.

2nd Cit.   Ay!   I'm on coming,
But not so hastily.   There's time enough.

The Workman.   Well, I have told you that there is
      scarce room.
I shall not tarry.ᵢ |*He hurries out*

2nd Cit. Why, what a strange turmoil!
And all about a simple heretic.

Enter three Market Girls *together.*

1*st Market Girl to* 2*nd Market Girl.* Have you heard
    the Duke of Lancaster intends
To come to the trial and defend the priest?

2nd M. G. No, but I'm glad. There will be much to
    see.

3rd M. G. It's in the Lady Chapel, do you know?

1*st M. G.* Oh! then we sha'n't see much. It is so small,
And every one is going. How I wish
I were a man!

        [*The bell of St. Paul's begins to toll, and con-*
          tinues through the scene.

2nd M. G. We sha'n't see much, that's true.

3rd M. G. They say the people are going in already,
And they will not begin till eight o' the clock.

2nd M. G. We shall have long to wait; but come along.
                          [*They go out.*
        Enter some Priests.

1*st Priest.* He has no chance. The bishops are against
    him.

2nd Priest. Perhaps he will convert them with his
    speech.

3rd Priest. Ay! that's certain. He's monstrous quick
    o' the tongue.

1*st P.* I wonder what his arguments will be.

2nd P. Oh! he has told them forth a thousand times,
He has no need of new ones

3rd P. Nay, that's so.

But we must hurry now, the minutes are flying.

  2nd P.   Let's keep together.

                                              [They go out.

                 City Officers *enter.*

  1st City Officer.   What did he say to ⟨you when first
you told him
The Duke of Lancaster would bring his men
And keep them round him ?

  2nd City O.   He pooh-poohed me forth,
Told me the Duke would never dare to do it,
And that it was a scare to frighten us.

  3rd City O.   He will not do it.

  1st City O.   Nay, that we shall see ;
But yet I wonder that we have no orders.
It would be better not to be too far
If we were needed.

  2nd City O.   Nay, I shall go to see,
And not keep order.

  3rd City O.   And I shall surely go.

                                   [They go out.

     The three Market Girls *returning arm-in-arm.*

  1st M. G.   Oh! what a shame that we could not get in
For all our going so early !   Now I wish,
And wish even doubly, that I were a man !

  2nd M. G.   Oh no you don't !   For then you could not
notice
Which of them you liked best, but you would be
For ever fighting.

  1st M. G.   Yes, indeed 1 do.

  Some more Market Girls *come in, as though going to St. Paul's.*

3rd M. G. No! No! you're all too late.   The church is
   full,
And we have been, and could not find an inch
To stand on!
   2nd Group.   Oh, the shame!
   1st Group.   It's no use going.
   2nd G.   Are you really sure?
   1st G.   Well, we have been.
   One of the 2nd G.   Then I suppose it really is no use?
But I *am* sorry.

                              [*They go out.*

SCENE II.

*St. Paul's Cathedral.   In the background is the door leading into
   the Lady Chapel.   The Cathedral is crowded.   The bells still
   sounding, but quicker.*

   A Man.   How long before the trial?
   Another.   Why, not long now.
   1st Man.   I wish that they would come; I'm tired of
      standing,
And yet I want to see him.   Do you think
'Tis certain he will enter by this way?
   2nd Man.   Well no, not certain; for the scheming Duke,
They say, has fixed to bring him; and 'tis certain
The Bishops will not let that old fox in
By their own entrance.   Here's a bishop coming.

              [*The* BISHOP OF LONDON *enters.   The crowd
                 press back so as to make room for him to kneel
                 as he passes towards and through the door of
                 the Lady Chapel.   He blesses them as he passes.*

   1st Man.   A saintly man.
   2nd Man.   Ay! that he is indeed.

His blessing does one good; and he's our bishop.

—Why does not Wiclif come?

1st Man.   He must come soon; the bishops are
assembled.

> [*Distant murmurs and shouts are heard.*

Ah! here he comes.   Do you not hear the shouts?

2nd Man.   Ay! and some murmurs; those must be
for the Duke.

> [*The noise increases.   The bell stops.*

1st. Man.   Now then he's at the door.   Why, what is this?
The people bar his entrance.

2nd Man.   No, the Duke's.

1st Man.   Ay!   That is so.   Then let him stand without.

2nd Man.   But Wiclif's with him.

1st Man.   Little credit then,
That such a saint should join with such a sinner.

> [*The* LORD MARSHAL'S *voice is heard.*

The Lord Marshal.   Ho! let me pass.   Make room
there!   Where's the way?

Make room, I say!

A voice.   Ay! let the Duke come in.

Lord M.   Do you not hear me?   Wiclif stands without.

A voice.   Ay! that's another matter.   Room there now!

Another.   Though I would give him little.

Another.   Nay, nor 1.

Enter the DUKE, *having at his side* WICLIF, *and preceded by* LORD
HENRY PERCY, *Grand Marshal of England.   He is followed
by a body of armed men and by five* Bachelors of Divinity *of
the five Mendicant Orders.*

Lord M.   Ho, there!   Make way!   Make way, I say,
and quick!

What do you here thus to prevent our path ?

A voice (from the back).   The church is free.

Lord M.   This is no church to-day,
But a judgment-hall where many souls are damned.

A voice.   Ay ! I know some among them.

The Lord M.   Now, make way.

> [*The* DUKE OF LANCASTER *and* WICLIF *follow.*
> *They proceed forward with difficulty.   Great*
> *mistrust is shown for the* DUKE, *and much*
> *respect, to* WICLIF.   *The people press on the*
> DUKE.

Duke.   Did you touch me, sirrah ?

Lord M. (conciliatingly).   Now, make room for us.

A man (to his neighbour).   Ay, that is better.   We do
not want his threats.

Lord M.   Stand back there, vassals !   The Duke has
need to pass.

A voice.   We are no vassals ; use you better terms.

Lord M.   Stand back, I tell you !

A man.   Why should I ?

Lord M. (pointing to the armed men).   These shall tell
you.

One of the crowd.   So ho ! to arms !   That's fit for one
in church !

> [*The' armed* Soldiers *come forward and clear a*
> *passage.   There is much noise.   After some*
> *resistance the armed men make a passage, and*
> *the* DUKE, *the* GRAND MARSHAL, WICLIF,
> *and five* Bachelors of Divinity *of the five*
> *Mendicant Orders pass through the door.   The*
> *people try to follow.*

SCENE III.

The Lady Chapel of St. Paul's Cathedral. The BISHOP OF
LONDON *and the rest of Convocation seated on raised seats in
their robes. Opposite them stands* WICLIF, *supported on either
side by the* DUKE OF LANCASTER, *and* LORD HENRY PERCY,
*Grand Marshal of England, together with his followers. The
rest of the Chapel is filled with monks, nobles, and citizens.*

Bishop. I greet you, noble Duke of Lancaster ;
I could have wished that you had come to-day
More quickly and as beseemed the place
We meet within.

Duke.   I bid you take again
The greeting that you gave me. As for these,

> [*Pointing to the armed men.*

When 'tis not safe to travel all alone,
Then we provide outriders,—such are these.

Bishop. Lord Marshal, was that not your voice with-
   out
Leading your strange processions to this building
With such unknown remark ?

Lord M.   It was, your Grace,
Done with intention. Are you answered now ?

Bishop. By Heaven ! How you love to play the
   Master !

Duke (aside). And we will be that which we love to
   play.

Bishop. It seems you were forgetful where you were.

Lord M. Where said you ?

Bishop.   In God's house.

Duke.   —God's judgment hall
Where priests and laymen should be held alike.—
(*Aside*) A prelate shall not rule the Duke this time.—
(*Aloud*) I always thought the doors of a judgment hall
Were free to all alike ; but now, it seems,
Your party, my Lord Bishop, has the power
And full monopoly of grace therein,
If you may come and our side may not come
To judge this man here now on heresy,
My friend through many years.
   Bishop.   I ask your Grace,
Is not this place God's house ?
   Duke.   God's house I know.
'Tis ye I know not.
                [*He points to the members of Convocation.*

   Bishop.   And shall quickly know,
Whoever's son you be.   Hear me, your Grace.
To this same see have I been consecrate,
And what I took so whole from those before me
Will I not hand to others violated.
I tell your Grace that I am Lord, not you,
Within these walls ; and therefore had I known
How the Lord Marshal would have carried him,
Rather than suffer such things at his hands,
I would have closed the doors upon his face.
It is not good to use God's Prelates so.
   Duke.   God's prelates !   Pope's procurers, sycophants
Remember, my Lord Bishop, who you are.
   Bishop.   I do.

Duke.   Remember, too, Lord Henry Percy
Is the Grand Marshal of all England.
   Bishop.   That do I not forget.
   Duke.   Neither forget
That you are subjects to the King of England,
And we are his vicegerents.   I will be
The master in this place in spite of you.
   A Citizen.   Did you hear that ?
   2nd Cit.   I did.
   3rd Cit.   He meant it, too.
There will be blood before we leave the church.
   1st Cit.   Ay ! that is likely—

           [LORD HENRY PERCY *rises, as though to speak.*

                  Hear Lord Percy now.
   2nd Cit.   *He* will not calm the waters.
   Lord Henry.   I call upon
This day's defendant now to seat himself,
For he has need of rest.   There will be much
That he will have to answer.   I pray you now
Be seated, Master Wiclif.
   Bishop.   What is this !
Be seated, in our presence, at the bar ?
I dare him to it.   And you, my good Lord Marshal,
Should be instilled with more discretion
Than thus to bid the prisoner seat himself.
   Lord H.   I say again I bid him to be seated.
   Bishop.   That shall not be, e'en though I die for it.
It is not meet when called before his judges ;

Nay, and not lawful either, for him so to sit
Within the court.

Lord H.   Lord Bishop, he shall sit.
Unnatural man to bid the prisoner stand,
Who hath more need of rest than all of you—
(*Aside*) Bishops and spiritual wickedness
In lofty places.

Bishop.   What was that you said?

Lord H.   I talked of spiritual wickedness
In lofty places.

Bishop.   Mother of God! to hear
Such speeches in our chapel.

Lord H.   Babylon!

Bishop.   Thou impious man!

Lord H.   Impiety is common.

Bishop.   I will not bear it!

Lord H.   No one pressed you to.

Bishop.   Temple profaner! Yet the voice of God—

Duke (*breaking in*). Enough! Enough! I say to
    you, enough!

Bishop.   I will be heard within my chapel here.
The State is great, but Church is over State.

Duke.   But shall not so continue. That I know.

Bishop.   The devil always had the stronger hand.

Duke.   Then is the Church the devil—you have said it!

Bishop.   The devil is in you; would it were the Church!

Duke.   Then were it made the worser! Ha, a hit!

Bishop.   Your words are big, but will not long be so.

Duke.   For words shall pass to action, so beware.

Bishop.   What ! do you threaten ?   Did I hear aright ?

Duke.   For arrogance is cumbered with a whip.

Bishop.   Am I then arrogant ?   Are Prelates so ?

Duke.   If that is so, all Prelates shall be whipped.
Ay ! and they shall be, William Courtenay.

Bishop.   If Prelates fail yet Courtenays may conquer.

Duke.   Be not too sure !   The Courtenays will have
Enough to answer for in their own selves,
With no regard to bishops.

Bishop.   Sooth to say,
If I may speak the truth, I place no trust
In Courtenays or any other name :—
God is my trust alone.

  The Duke (in a low voice to LORD PERCY).   By Heaven
        I say,
Rather than swallow such affront as that,
I soon will drag the boasting bishop forth
From out the church by his own saintly hair !

A Citizen.   Did you hear that ?

2nd Cit.   I did.

3rd Cit.   And so did I.
By Lady Mary, he has gone too far !

1st Cit.   We must not let him treat our bishop so.

2nd Cit.   And will not.

A voice.   Save the bishop !

2nd voice.   Ay ! to arms.

Duke.   To arms, then would you ?   Then defend your-
        selves.

Bishop (rising).   Hear, citizens of London, this hath gone

                                                5

So far to-day that now the ordered trial
Must be postponed. It is impossible
To measure justice where injustice rules.

   Duke. Ay! well said, Bishop! Therefore lead the
     way.

   Bishop. Owing to what the Duke of Lancaster,
And all his satellites that are with him,
Have said and done within the court to-day,
We do postpone this trial till some date
Hereafter to be settled. The court is over.

> [*The* BISHOP *and the other judges rise and go out by
> a private door into the Chapter House. Much
> commotion and menaces against the* DUKE,
> *who goes out with the* LORD MARSHAL *by
> the other door.* WICLIF, *attended by a strong
> guard, accompanies him.*

   1st Cit. What think you, Master Humphrey, of the
     trial?

   2nd Cit. The end hath not come yet. There's more to
     follow.

   1st Cit. The Duke is in the wrong; that's clear to see.

   3rd Cit. Ay! we will teach him better words than
     that.

   2nd Cit. Yea! and right soon. Let's follow to his
     palace.

   1st Cit. Where has he gone?

   3rd Cit.　　　　　　　　　　Why, back to the Savoy.

   2nd Cit. Then will we follow. Burghers, follow us!
To the Savoy!

   The crowd.　　　Ay! lead. To the Savoy!

SCENE IV.

A street in London *near St. Paul's.* Citizens *entering.*

1st Cit.   Which way went the Duke?

2nd Cit.   Nay, that I know not.

3rd Cit.   His barge was waiting down there by the
Tower.

1st Cit.   Then that way went he.

2nd Cit.   Nay, they were too many;
He would not dare to leave the half behind
To brave our vengeance.

3rd Cit.   Ay!   That's sure enough.

1st Cit.   Then have they gone back straight to the
Savoy,
Where we as straightly now will follow him.
What say you?

2nd Cit.   Ay, let us follow.

1st Cit.   Speak forth then,
How many now will dare to follow me
To brave the lion in his palace-den?

Citizens.   All, all of us!   Lead on, we'll follow you.

Enter an Old Citizen.

O. Cit.   What would you, masters?

Cits.   Why, fetch out the Duke
For the great insult that he laid upon
Our Bishop.   Ay!   There'll be some fun!

O. Cit.   What would you?   Sack the palace?

Cits.   Very like.

O. Cit.   Nay, do that not.   Be warned by me in time.

A voice.   We hear you, dotard.

O. Cit.   Dotards oft speak true

When striplings err, however fine their wits.

I bid you, pray you, masters, to desist.

You will gain nothing.

   A voice.   Ay ! that we shall see.

   O. Cit.   Well, well ; I cannot stay you.

   Cits.   Come with us !

   O. Cit.   Nay, nay ! I am too old.   I stay at home.

Enter another body of Citizens *rushing in.*

   2nd Cits.   Shame, shame ! we will not bear it !

   1st Cits.   What has happened ?

   2nd Cits.   Why, Robert Conmore has been put in
      chains

For no offence whatever.

   1st Cits.   Who has done it ?

   2nd Cits.   The Lord Marshal in his city house !

   1st Cits. (a group).   Off to Lord Percy's !

   2nd Cits.   Yea !   And worse has happened !

The Lord Mayor is prohibited from his office,

And in his stead, as Royal Commissioner,

The imprisoned Latimer !

   1st Cits.   Then let us go

And liberate the prisoner from his house ;

Your Latimers can wait.

   2nd Cits.   So to Lord Percy's.

   1st Cits.   The rest to the Savoy.   We'll catch them yet.

SCENE V.

The Gatehouse before the mansion of the DUKE OF LANCASTER *in the Savoy, a few* Soldiers *of the* DUKE'S *within. The burghers in tumult. More* Citizens *entering.*

1st Cit.   Is the lion in lair?

2nd Cit.   We know not, but it seems so.

1st Cit.   And where's the jackal, his companion?
We searched for him where he in general lives,
But he had fled, no doubt for safety here.

A group of Market-Girls *enter and cross the stage, calling to* Citizens *behind.*

1st Market-Girl.   Come along, citizens! here's the old
      thief's den.
Now let him know he should not spoil our treats.

More Citizens *enter.*

1st Cit. Yes, here he is; that will I warrant for.

                 [*Calling to the* Soldiers *in the Gatehouse.*

Ho! Master Haughty, is the villain in?

Soldier (from the walls).   Whom call you villain?
      'Twere as well for you
To use more caution when you speak to us.

2nd Cit.   What! Does he threaten us? Then down
      with him!

                            [*A stone is thrown.*

Soldier.   I am a soldier of the Duke's within,
It were as well to show him more respect.

Citizens.   Ay! we do know your master, otherwise
We should not now be treating thus with you.

            [*Another stone is thrown, hitting the soldier.*

Soldier. Ho! Is that so? Guard there, to arms!
The people do assault the Gatehouse here.

Cits. Ay then, to arms! to arms! Now stand together.
They cannot harm us with their pikes up there.

> [*Several* Soldiers *appear on the wall. The* Citizens
> *bring a huge beam and batter in the gate.*

Now we will show him how to treat our bishop!
Down with the gates! A stroke, and it is done!
Now then, another! Stand up to the task!

> [*A plank in the door flies. The* Soldiers *on the
> gate run off into the mansion, the drawbridge
> goes up.*

Ha! we have won the Gatehouse. They have fled
Like doves before an eagle to the mansion!
Follow, ay, follow! Ah, it is too late!
What shall we do, we cannot reach him now?

A voice. Span o'er the moat!

Cits.   It is too broad!

> [*The portcullis is let down*

                              See now
They have let down the iron portcullis-work.
There is no reaching them when that is down.

Other Cits. No! And besides, there are soldiers there
    within
Well armed, and we are armless.

A group.   Yes! There are soldiers.

> [*They espy the* DUKE OF LANCASTER'S *coat-of-
> arms hanging up on the wall within the
> Gatehouse.*

A Cit. The Duke of Lancaster!

Cits.   Where? Tell us, where?

A Cit. Why, there, upon the wall in effigy—
At least his coat-of-arms, which is as good!

Cits. Down with the Duke! The Duke in effigy!
Who left his coat-of-arms out here to dry?
Quick, get it down!

> [*A youth runs up with a jumping pole.*

A Cit.   Ah! Here's the boy for us!
Now we will have it!

> [*He dislodges the coat-of-arms with the pole.*

                    Ha! The coat is fallen!

Cits. Tramble it under foot!

A group.   No, no! Preserve it.
It will be good perhaps for hunter's marks.

> [*They drag it out through the gateway.*

Cits. What shall we do with it?

A Cit.   Ah, now I have it!

Cits. What do you propose?

A Cit.   Where is the pole
With which we reached it down?

> [*They show it him.*

                    Why, here it is!
Now clear a place within the middle here.
We will reset him here but in disgrace,
Like Holy Peter, with his head turned downwards.

Cits. Good, good! Folks, clear a space. This place
  were best.

> [*The* Citizen *puts it on the pole reversed, and fixes
> the pole in the ground.*

A Cit. So would we do had we the Duke himself.

Another Cit. I wish it were he! I would give him this.

> [*He throws a clod at the coat-of-arms.*

Cits. See to the drawbridge! Some one has come out!

> [*The drawbridge of the palace is let down, and a*
> Mendicant Monk *comes out.*

Ho, Toll-pate! Is the Duke at Mass? What news?

Monk. Good people, go away in quietude;
You have disturbed the Duke with all this noise.

A Cit. "Disturbed" him—ay! "disturbed" him, did
  you say?
That's what the murder said of the murderer!
Inform the Duke that 'tis he that does disturb us.

Cits. Yea! back, old goose-quill!

A group.   Not too quickly, though!
Let him be placed beside the effigy,
A worthy answer to the insult given!
Why did you follow in the ducal train?
Are you for him?

Monk.   Nay, I am not against him!

Cits. "Who is not for us is against us," now.

A group. We will keep the monk, but let the man go free!

> [*They strip him of his monastic dress.*

Monk. Help, help! The Church is here in danger.

> [*He runs out.*

[*Enter* WILLIAM COURTENAY, Bishop of London, *with a few*
Attendants.

Cits. Room for the Bishop. See, his Grace approaches.

> [*He takes up a position in front of the stage.*

London. Good people, what now would you, with this
    tumult ?

A Cit. Our Bishop was insulted in St. Paul's,
And we do love our Bishop.

London.   Much I thank you
For your devotion to our sacred office—
Yet slowly, slowly ! What did that man here
Who ran and cried, " The Church is here in danger " ?

The Group. Your Grace, he was a brutal mendicant
Who followed on the Duke this very morning.
We took his robe, but let the man escape.

Lon. It was not well. He was a priestly man.
See, how, though thus jealous for the Church,
You do transgress her sacred ordinance,
By pillaging some priestly mendicants !
Fie ! Such is not the way that you should work.

Cits. If we did do what you would hold not well
We are repaid with our own felt remorse.
What would you have us do ?

Lon.   To-day enough
Has been returned for evils of the Duke's.
See, you make insult on his coat-of-arms
And plunder his dear priests. That is enough.
Disperse now, for the day grows very late.
The Duke will not forget your deeds to-day.
Say, are you willing ?

Cits.   When your Grace commands
We must obey. Your wishes are commands.
Therefore must we obey you in this matter.

Lon.   There's my good people ! Now then, all disperse.

> [*The* Citizens *begin to go out.* *The* BISHOP *also.*

Do not forget the Bishop is your friend !
You may have need of many yet awhile.

> [*He goes out.*

Scene VI.

The same as before. Citizens, *etc.* *Enter* WICLIF.

1st Cit.   Are you not Master Wiclif ?
Wic.   I know no other.
A voice.   This man was with the Duke of Lancaster !
Wic.   What would you, friend ?
A voice.   He did insult our Bishop.
Wic.   Would he had not !
1st Cit. (coming forward).   Now, mark me, Master Wiclif.
We burghers wish that all men should be free
Who come among us.   Therefore are you free.
But have a care.   He who enjoys our freedom
Must keep himself within our city's laws.
Your master did abuse those laws to-day.

Wic.   " My master," did you say ?   I know but One,
And He is not of this world.
A voice.   John of Gaunt,
The Duke of Lancaster—he is your master !

Wic.   Master have I none but only Christ.
That I did come with this same Duke of Lancaster
Is my misfortune, since he acted so.

1st Cit.   Now mark me, Master Wiclif ! We in London
Do love you and your principles ; but see

Lest men for their own ends should prostitute
Your firm belief. I speak for your advice.
Speak out, and then we burghers follow you.
You saw how all the city crowded there
To hear you in defence against the Bishop.
Both are our friends, but that the Bishop
Doth make too much of his authority.
But all these things do we forget when insult
By royal dukes is brought against his head.
Now mark me, Master Wiclif, what I say.

Wic. My friend, I thank you for your courtesy.
And all you burghers I may call my friends,
Seeing I fight for you.

   A Citizen (*pointing to the coat-of-arms*). *He* fought
     against us.

Wic. My cause is not the Duke of Lancaster's.
That he did so insult your noble Bishop
I sorrow much.   In token of the same

     [*Taking hold of the pole, and shaking down the
      coat-of-arms.*

See, I do trample on his coat-of-arms ;
Who takes to force, shall be repelled by force.

   A Cit. See ! He hath joined our cause against the
     Duke !

Wic. My friends, I do no harm.   What I have done
Is done to show I blame what he has done.

   A voice. Who takes to force, shall be repelled by force !

   1st Cit. Now mark me, Master Wiclif !   Have a care.
It is not well to barter with the great.

They do but use you for ill purposes,

Though all the while concealing their base ends.

It is not well to barter with the great.

I tell thee, Master Wiclif, have a care !

 Wic. Friend ! Yea, my friend ! I thank you for your
  council.

When I am next accused I stand alone.

 1st Cit. (coming forward, and taking his hand). No,
  you do not. For we do stand with you.

 Cit. Yes, you do fight for freedom ! We are with you.

 Wic. My friends ! I thank you from my very heart.

           [*The curtain falls.*

Scene VII.

A room in the Archbishop's *Palace at* Lambeth. *The* Archbishop
of Canterbury *and the* Bishop of London.

 London. Your Grace, it was so. Already had fallen down

The battlements, the gates already given ;

The palace would have been sacked had not myself,

Their Bishop, placed me at their head that day,

To stop the fray, and further damage done.

The people hate him. There shall be no king

Whose name is John, they say,—ay ! some on oath.

Who do they mean, if not this Lancaster ?

 Canterbury. Then are the people with us, and the King

Has said expressly, Richard must be King,

His grandson.

(*After a pause.*) Where was Wiclif in the fray ?

Did he do aught to stay the populace ?

Lon. Ay, that did he.   He was at first, methinks,
With Lancaster, within the palace walls.
But when he saw the people how they stirred,
Either the Duke dismissed him, or he went
Of his own will among the people there,
And tried to stay them from their holy rage
Against his royal protector, but in vain.
They stormed at him like Grecians after war
Against a general who met defeat.
So went he crestfallen upon his way.

Can. Oh, he is dangerous, and must be stayed !
And therefore am I glad that now have come
The Papal bulls from Rome, which we did ask for.
Now will we stay him.   One is to the King,
And three to us, that we should ascertain
Whether the doctrines which are heretic
Are truly preached by Wiclif, and to guard
Against absconsion by the heretic,
If haply he should hear of our intent.
The third commands that Wiclif should be tried
By judges competent, and well inclined,
And that the King and all the royal court
Should be informed of his misdeeds and words,
So that they should not shelter one by law cast out.
The last is to the Chancellor of Oxford,
That he may be detained.

Lon.   This must be done
With quickness.   Should the King, who is so sick,
And like to die, depart before 'tis done,

Then must we wait for many further months,
For newer bulls and fresher ordinance.

   Can. Ay! that is so; and therefore have I sent
These presents to their owners in hot haste.

   Lon. It was well done!

Enter the BISHOP OF ROCHESTER *hurriedly, and with agitation.*

   Rochester. Greeting, my brothers in Christ!

   Can. You are disturbed? What is it makes you so?

   Roch. Your Grace, I posted hither straight from Sheen.
The King is worse, and seemly like to die,
The noble courtiers are denied his presence,
And no one but the leman, Alice Perrers,
Approaches to his person. I did think
Perhaps the time was come for you to go
And minister to him the Sacrament
Before he dies. He cannot last a day,
The King's physician told me so himself.

   Lon. It is high time to stir. For who can tell,
It may be that the Duke will somehow act
Upon his weakened will to be yet named
To fill the vacant throne?

   Can.   Ay! I must go.
I would so grand a monarch should die better
Than in a leman's arms. If that is so,
Too few will dare to stand beside his bed
And do his orders, or receive his words.
Ay! it is time to go.

               [*To the* BISHOP OF LONDON, *taking his hand.*
Do you come too?

Lon. If so it please your Grace !

Can. Then come with me.

[*Turning to the* BISHOP OF ROCHESTER.

And you, our brother, do you stay behind ?

Roch. I wait your Grace's wish.

Can. Then come with us,

There cannot be too many where he dies.
Let us pay honour when a King departs
Who once has been a hero.

[*They go out.*

SCENE VIII.

A room in the DUKE OF LANCASTER'S *mansion in the* Savoy. *The*
DUKE *alone. He holds a despatch in his hand, which he is*
reading.

The Duke. " *The King, who has been daily growing*
weaker, is sinking now at last, and cannot last till morn.
He may be dead before you receive this, for his life hangs
merely on a thread. Therefore be prepared, for you know
that the first blow often decides the event."

King, or no king ? Prince, or the highest prince ?—
And in a day's length settled. We must wait.
The jewelled crown, which we ourselves do seek,
May yet be placed by other loyal hands
Upon our head. The vista widens out.
The minutes linger now when they should speed.
I am alone. Princes are aye alone,
And kings still lonelier. That's like a king.
O God ! how unsubdued I feel to-day,

And all unbrotherly.   The demon calls.
The people hate me, that I do believe.
They shall not hate when I become their king.
If so it shall be.   Lady ! let them hate
So long as I shall reign.   King John, King John—
Yet I had wished a name less ominous
Than to be second after such a first—
A weakling server.   Ay ! the name shall be
Better than that—if name it be at all.
I could be great, although they hate me so ;
I would be great, because they hate me so ;
And strive to cure the hate which they do bear me
By kinder rule and juster attributes.
A court as pure and purer still than this,
And justice done through England's length and breadth,
With England's name held up in the clear sky,
As subjected to no one.   Yet the King
May rally yet ; he has been long a-dying.
But now the years seem fully ripe in him
Who fills the throne of kings.   One more, one more,
And only one between the throne and me.
Whoe'er can tell ?   Upon so small a thread
Hangs human life, it may be yet that I,
By merely waiting, shall arrive at what
I so desire, and with no evil done.
Yet little Richard !   He should be our king,
My brother's offspring.   Oh, Heredity !
With what fierce malice is your ruling fraught,
And how thou harmest all thou look'st upon !

To fight and be a king, or rest a slave,
Which were the better ?   Rather, which one choose ?—
Oh, for some light upon this misty road !
[He pauses.
Ha, ha ! I have it.   I will to the King,
'Tis not too late to set aside the boy ;
Yet is there time, and I will post forthwith.
The King that was shall dub me King to be,—
Yet will I be their King,—
[A bell tolls.
—What bell was that ?
It had an ominous note, and flushes me.
[He pauses.   The bell tolls again.
Again the bell !   It does not augur well.
*[He opens a window and looks out.   The bell keeps
tolling.*
The citizens are crowding in the streets,
Their looks seem clouded.   Something is at hand ;
I like it not.
[Calling to the Attendants *within.*
What ho !   What ho, without !
Enter an Attendant, *who appears agitated.*
Your steps are slow ; why are you thus distraught ?
I called you twice.
[The bell sounds.
Wherefore is that bell ?
[The Attendant *is silent.*
And why this crowding in the open streets ?
*[The people without are heard, at first softly, but
ever louder and louder shouting.*

6

Attendant.   Your Grace, a messenger has come from
     Sheen—

Lan.   Enough, enough!

> [*He stands as though about to fall, then listens to
> the voices in the street.*

Voices.   Long live the King, King Richard!
We will have none but Richard!

> [*The* DUKE *falls fainting in a chair.*

Lan.   It is too late!

> [*The curtain falls.*

SCENE IX.

WICLIF'S *lodging in* London. *In the background an open window
     looking into the street.   It is summer time, and roses are twin-
     ing round the window.* WICLIF *alone.*

Wiclif.   Across the sky a tiny star may go
Upon its path, and heedless that it makes
The toiling sailor surer of his home,
Trimming his ship by marking of its light.
A noble star that does not stop to think
If it's observed how well he shines by night!
So must my path be through the darkened world.
Lord, shine upon me, fill me with Thy light,
As now Thy sun doth fill this other world.
I would my way was open to my view,
But now I grope along it comfortless,
The future dark, the present all unsure.—
A little while, and then all will be o'er.

> [*A voice is heard singing from an inner room.*
> WICLIF *listens.*

Roses rare
　　Fill the earth :
Love was there,
　　At their birth,
Everywhere.

Thorn and flower
　　Make the rose ;
Sun and shower,
　　Mountain snows,
For man's dower.

Sorrows lie
　　At our feet ;
Pass them by,
　　Kiss me sweet,
Or I die.

Wic.　Now some one's heart is light within her body !

[*Calling.*

Is that you, Esther ?

Enter ESTHER.

Esther.　　　　　　　It was so, Master.

Wic.　　　　　　　　　　　　Good !

Who taught you to sing rhymes so fanciful
On such a running ?

Esther.　　　　　　Master, Master Horn,

When we were all at Oxford at the Hall :
He gave it to Mistress Janet.　She taught it me.
I crave your pardon if it did disturb you.

Wic.　Ah no ! ah no !　Have you heard of Mistress Janet?

Enter a Servant.

Servant.　There waits below a gentleman on you,
Who has come, he says, from far to find you here.
Shall he have entrance ?

Wic.   Let him come to me.

   [*The* Servant *goes out, and returns with* JANET,
     who is disguised as a traveller. *The* Servant
     and ESTHER *leave them.*

Jan.   You do not know me ?

Wic.   Your voice I seem to know,
But figure not.   No ; I cannot say I know you.

Jan.   And yet you should do.   Will you think again ?

Wic.   Forgive me, sir, I cannot say I know you.

Jan.   Your memory is short.   I give you help.
I come from Lutterworth.

Wic.   From Lutterworth
The voice would come which I do seem to know.
You bring me news of Janet, my own niece ?
Perhaps you do not know her ?

Jan.   (*disclosing herself*).   I am she !

   [*As she rushes towards him and he embraces her.*

Wic.   My own brave girl !   What maiden's jest is this ?
What have you done, and wherefore are you here ?

Jan.   They said you were in danger in the town,
And all alone.   I come to tend to you.

Wic.   My darling Janet !   How then did you dare
To travel thus so far, so all alone
Amidst the dangers which beset your way ?

Jan.   I am your niece !   You ask me how I dare ?
Are lessons taught for such vain purposes ?
Uncle, I come to tender to your wants.
You are alone, and no one knows your needs—
Is not then that enough ?

Wic. (*kissing her*).   You are too brave.

Why! I shall gather braveness from your strength.—

'Tis not so hard to fight when not alone.

Jan.   To fight, my father!   Will they stay you yet?

They told me you were safe from them by now,

Being saved by the help of many men of weight.

Wic.   That is quite true.

Jan.   Then wherefore must you fight?

Wic.   Life, life!   Janet, we men were made to fight.

The Duke for his own ends protected me.

Then when the old King died and left the crown

To our boy-monarch for his heritage,

And when the people did accept the boy—

Pfiff! we hear no more of Lancaster.

The Bishops, as I hear, intend again

To aim at me with missiles from the Pope—

Because, forsooth, I preach to them the Truth!—

[Stroking her head.

'Tis not so hard to fight when not alone!

Jan.   My own brave father!   How I honour you!

Wic.   How did you find the folk at Lutterworth?

Jan.   Why, all for you, as they indeed should be.

I could not say my uncle is in danger,

But they would curse the Bishops and the Pope!

Wic.   There England's strength doth lie—among her
    people.

Enter a Servant.

Servant.   A stranger waits without who wants to see
    you.

Wic. What ! Still another ? Prithee, ask of him
His name, his business, and whence he hath come.

> [*The* Servant *goes out.*

He will be startled if he see you thus,
Half man, half woman,—
What will you do ?

> *The* Servant *re-enters.*

Ser. The stranger doth send word
His name is Horn. He comes from Oxford here.
He says you know his business.

Jan. (*turning pale*). Holy Mary !
He must not find me here. What shall I do ?
Ah ! yet I have it.

> [*She seizes her mantle, and robes herself as at first.*
> *To* WICLIF.

—Uncle, favour me,
And let me stay with you a little while
Still as the stranger.

Wic. Well, love, as you will.

> [*To the* Servant.

Tell him that I have leisure, and will see him now.

> [*The* Servant *goes out.*

I wonder what he does here in the city ?

Jan. (*aside slowly*). I wonder what he thinks of one
within it.

> [*A short pause. Then enter* Servant, *followed by*
> JOHN HORN, *dressed as a young monk.*

Ser. He is before you.

Wic. (*to the* Servant).   You can leave us now.

> [*The* Servant *goes out.*

Horn.   O Master !

> [*Rushes forward, and, seizing* WICLIF'S *hand, he kneels down and kisses it.*

Wic.   So you still remember me ?

Horn.   And should I not?   Old teachers are old friends.

Wic.   It is not all old pupils find them out,
To greet them when they meet adversity.
But yet you are not all alone to-day,—
See, there is yet another in the room
Who has come to cheer me.

> [HORN *looks round and discovers* JANET, *without recognising her. He rises hastily, and makes a deep bow to her.*

Horn.   I had not noticed him.
He will forgive me that I greeted you
Perhaps with more affection than I should.
But had he known and loved, as I have done,
Both you and yours, he would not think it strange.
(*To Janet.*)   I was a pupil of my master here
Some time ago in Oxford.

Jan.   So was I.

Horn.   I do not know your face as one of them.

Jan.   Yet I knew the Warden and his household too.

Horn.   You knew the household ?   Then you knew the niece ?

Wic. The stranger came from Lutterworth to-day.

Horn.   Ah ! then you know her better than I thought.

Jan.   I cannot say that I have ever seen her.

Horn.   And yet you knew the master's family !

Jan.   What is she like ?

Horn.   About as tall as you,
And somewhat so complexioned.   But her hair
Hung down in golden tresses on her back.

Jan.   You speak of her with somewhat ferventness.

Horn.   Oh no !   She was a pleasing little thing.

Jan.   You did not love her then ?   I thought you did.

Horn. Well, there was something so between us, true !

Jan.   Not very much, but just enough for teasing ?

Horn.   Ah ! now you press me ; and you are, I think,
A little too inquisitive.

Jan.   Dear sir,
I ask your pardon if I have offended.
I *have* heard the country people talk of her.

Wic.   My niece is here in London at this moment
Of whom you talk.

Horn (*startled*).   My master, where ?

Jan. (*throwing off her disguise*).   Before you !
                    [*Rushing towards her as to* WICLIF *before.*

Horn.   Oh, Janet !

Jan.   Say, " a pleasing little thing,"
And then, " well, true, something there was between us."
                              [*Imitating him.*

Horn.   Oh, you are cruel !   Would you have me speak
To one a stranger of your uncle's niece ?

Wic.   But now, come, tell me why you are come here ?

Horn.   Master, you are in danger, and you ask ?

The terms of my noviciate were done,
And I had heard you were in trouble here,
Being set upon by Bishops and the Pope,
And losing in the dead your patronage.
Master, I came, in short, to succour you
With what small help is mine.
   Wic.   Oh, nobly planned!
I do deserve to have great strength indeed,
Being thus befriended in the hour of need.
My children, ye are both come here to nurse me.
I give you what I may—an old man's blessing.
But now I go to tell the good folk here
Of your arrival. Our small family
Will need still yet awhile some kindly shelter
Against the cold.
   Jan.   Then, uncle, let me go.
   Wic. (*laughing*). What! Thus arrayed?
   Jan. (*laughing also*).   I had forgot my suit.
                 [WICLIF *goes out.*

   Horn. It is a long time since we met before.
   Jan. Yes, you are altered much since that last time—
Older and somewhat priestlier, are you not?
   Horn. Man's intellect grows older and more learned,
His heart is ever young and cleverest most
When young in years.
   Jan.   Then you have lost in heart
What you have gained in head. Is it so you mean?
   Horn. I do hope not, else had I not gained much.—
You, too, are altered.

Jan.   Those that live must change.

Horn. Are you changed much?

Jan.   Some things can know no change;
And others, if they change not, must straight die;
While some love change, as some to keep unchanged,
You must not blame chameleons that they change,
Nor wonder if a sapphire changes not.

 Horn. I have more taste for jewels than for vermin.

 Jan. Jewels are worthless, vermin full of life.

 Horn. And full of hate; but jewels never change.

 Jan. You do not love then change?

 Horn.   Should I be here
If that was so?

 Jan.   I gave you once a rose
To put before your crucifix one day.

 Horn. (*drawing the flower from his breast*). And here
  it is. I have no heed of change.

 Jan. (*pausing awhile*). It is grown musty.

 Horn.   Still it is a rose.

 Jan. May I not go to get another one
To place beside it?

     [*She rises to go to the window, to pluck one of the
      roses.*

 Horn.   I need only one.

     [*He looks up into her face. Their eyes meet.*

Oh, all too lovely for my earthly days,
My rose which I have cherished in my breast
To strengthen and console me on my ways!

     [*Taking both her hands in his.*

Our eyes have met, and now our hands have met,
Shall not at last our lips in kisses meet,
Long-drawn and passionate, with love's fount wet ?

   Jan.   Love, have you loved me through these many days,
And I not known what love to me confessed
To strengthen and console me on my ways ?

                                              [*Kissing him.*

Our eyes, our hands, and now our lips have met.
You do believe I love you—do you, sweet ?
Then one kiss more that we may not forget.

                      [*During the last twelve lines strolling musicians*
                        have been heard playing, drawing gradually
                        nearer under the window. The music gets
                        louder and louder as they now approach under
                        the window. JOHN HORN *and* JANET *go to the*
                        window. Their voices are heard, the music
                        stopping.

   1st Mus.   Largess, my lady.   Give us of your wealth.

   2nd Mus.   The Lady Mary bless you, noble sir !
We ask a favour for your lady's sake.

   Jan. (*throwing them some money*).   There !   Take this
    trifle for his sake as well.

   Musicians.   We thank you, noble lady, noble sir.
The Lady Mary's blessing on you both.

                      [*The music recommences as they are heard to retire.*
                       JOHN HORN *and* JANET *return laughing, and*
                       hand-in-hand, into the room.

   Horn.   These poor musicians settled all for us !

   Jan.   When actors play 'tis not so hard to judge
How the play will finish.

Horn.   May it then end so.

                    [*Regarding her costume.*

Why !   But how strangely you are dressed the while !

                    [*Regarding herself, then him.*

Jan.   And you, Sir Lover, hardly seem right clad !
You, soon a monk ; and I, a stranger youth !
    Horn.   Yet made for one another, as it seems.
    Jan.   I have an uncle who has need of me.
    Horn.   I have a Master whom I mean to serve.
That can we do together, can we not ?
    Jan.   You are a monk, your service should be God's.
    Horn.   But you I love.   Does love not come from God ?
    Jan.   I love you.
    Horn.   And I love you—

                    Enter WICLIF.

Wic.   What is this ?
Still both together ?
    Jan.   —Father, we have been
A long, long way since you did leave us here.
    Wic.   And did not quarrel as you went along ?
    Horn.   That will I answer for.
    Wic.   Well, we shall see.
But now I come to bid you go with me.
I have prepared below a frugal meal;
You must be weary with your several rides.
Come then, my daughter.   Pupil, come with us.

                    [*They go out.   The curtain falls.*

SCENE X.

A room in the Palace at Lambeth. *The* ARCHBISHOP *alone.*

Archbishop. I should have had report before this time
From Oxford, how our message was received
By those in power. Ill omen is delay.
For it may be that there the old King's death
Hath changed men's fortunes, even as with us
In London round the palace. Much I fear
That those our enemies who are in office
Will seize upon this opportunity
To nullify the bull and the citations
As being rendered in the old King's name.
Such nuisance waits upon a monarch's death.
However, we must wait.

Enter a Servant.

Ah ! as I thought,—
A message now. You bring me news of what ?
Servant. Your Grace, a messenger has just arrived
From Oxford. Shall he have entrance ?
Arch.   Certainly,
For I await his message. Let him come.   .

[The Servant goes out.

Now shall I know the measure of success
Which may await us. Yet I fear the worst.
Where learning is, obstruction's sure to lurk.

Enter the Servant, followed by a Messenger.

Mess. Your Grace, I bring you message of reply
From Oxford, to the summons you had sent.

Arch. I trust that they received it favourably,
Seeing the name which that same summons bore ?
    Mess. Bear with me, good your Grace, if I should bear
News not so gracious as you might have wished,
And I, too, hoped for, being the messenger.
—Your Grace, I have to tell you in their name,
The council of the University,
In complete force assembled, has received
Your own citations and the Papal Bull.
And now, upon its full consideration,
Begging your Grace to pardon their decision,
As being with open conscience fixed upon,
Do now in my own person here refuse
To yield to Rome one of their own free body
Who hath done nought, so far as they are 'ware,
To merit such detention and compulsion.
As for the doctrines which this cleric holds,
These will they all examine in full time.—
You have my message.
    Arch. (*with rage*).   Would you had brought none,
It had been better for you and for them.
I will not let these prating clerics loose,
For they shall suffer for their negligence
In spreading thus abroad blank heresy.
    Mess. Your Grace, they have not any fixed upon
Their firm belief without first patient study
And holy prayer.
    Arch.   Prayer ! talk not to me thus.
'Tis something new when messengers must argue.

Do you keep silence.

Mess.   With your leave I will.

Arch.   He shall not thus escape me, well I know,
This Wiclif.   With my own express command
Shall he be summoned to the Palace here
To answer to these charges.   `
(*To the* Messenger.)   Leave me now.

> [*The* Messenger *goes out.*

Yet will we have him in our hold at last.
Methinks he will not have the Duke of Lancaster
To hold his shield before him and insult us.
This is our gain from circumstance.   Sometimes
A monarch's death is mightier than his life;
So this one's was in its last days of breath.
(*To the* Servant.)   Sirrah! inquire for me if it is known
Where Wiclif is.

Ser.   Your Grace, if I may speak,
It chances that I know he is in London at this time:
I know his lodging, close upon the Strand.

Arch.   Then have him straightway summoned to our
        Palace—
Or, stay!   Formality in this bears strength.
My hand shall write the summons on his own person.

> [*He writes.*

(*To the* Servant.)   Lest he should chance escape us, let
        it be seen
That this is carried forward faithfully.
You understand?

Serv.   I do, your Grace.

Arch.   Enough !

> [*The* Servant *goes out.*

He shall be tried in my own chapel here,
Before myself and my own brother,
William Courtenay, Bishop of St. Paul's.
It scarce can be that he shall now escape us.

> [*He goes out.   The curtain falls.*

Scene XI.

The Chapel in the Archbishop's *Palace at* Lambeth.   *On a raised dais,* Simon Sudbury, Archbishop of Canterbury, *and the* Bishops of London *and* Rochester, *right and left, a little lower.   The rest of the Chapel is occupied by the* Archbishop's *retainers and a few* Clerks, Monks, *and* Priests. Wiclif *stands before the dais alone.*

Archbishop.   There is no need to-day of words from me,
For all here know why we are thus assembled.
Therefore let our own officer proclaim
The charge against this man before us now.
May God have mercy on a damnèd soul !—
Read, officer, the charges brought against him.

Officer (reads).   "*John Wiclif, Rector now of Lutter-
worth,*
Lying within the Diocese of Lincoln,
And former Warden in the city of Oxford
Of that same body, Canterbury Hall,
Founded by Simon Islip, once Archbishop,
From which the same John ·Wiclif was expelled
For reasons various and manifold ;—

Is hereby summoned by our primate hand
To yield himself before his lawful judges,
Who are empowered, in matters spiritual,
In our own chapel within Lambeth Palace,
Within eight days, to answer certain charges
Which have been brought against him by the Pope
Upon the doctrine he is said to preach.
First, that he holds strange views upon the rights
Of property and of inheritance.
Second, upon the moneys of the Church,
Which he hath said may all be confiscate
·To purpose secular in time of need.
Third, on the power of the Church's discipline,
And on the limits which are necessary.
These, under nineteen counts which are here stated,
And which I now deliver unto you,
Are these same charges which you now must meet.
May God have mercy on an erring soul."

Arch.   Have you found aught to answer to us now
Against these charges which are herein named ?
An honest man would straight admit the truth.

Wiclif.   My lord and judges who are here assembled,
If I speak less to-day than I could wish,
Remember that you hear an agèd man,
Whose prime of life has many years gone by.
If I do speak what I may have to say
To-day, in fearlessness—that now forgive,
Not thinking that I reck not of your rank
As being my superiors in holy things,
And that I have forgotten who you are,

And where I am being brought before you now.
But man must speak the truth in fearlessness.
Therefore, remembering fully your estate,
And the full power which you have over me,
Shall I speak forth.   Nor do I now forget
That I am standing here before a throne
More sacred and more mighty than is this
Which is before me.   In God's sight I stand,
.Who hears my words, and will remember them
Against my coming on the Judgment Day.—
Before God's throne I stand, before the throne
Where you and I, made equal, shall one day,
Both sinners and both guilty, waiting stand
For judgment when the seals are broken through.
For man must speak the truth in fearlessness.
I stand, I say, before the throne of God,
For I do see engraved upon that throne
The words : "WHO SITS HEREON IS CALLÈD TRUTH."
Therefore I dare not lie, and would not lie,
For I do stand before the throne of Truth,
Which judges all at last.   My lords and judges,
I bid you bear with me if I have come,
After considering for many years,—
Which I have done with prayerful carefulness,—
To these conclusions which do please you not.
If they offend you, then the Truth offends—
Not I, who do but register the Truth.
Yea ! men must speak the truth in fearlessness.
Longer I will not keep you, if so be

You do allow to me and my old age
To give my answer here in written terms.

> [*He hands a paper to the* Officer.

This let the Pope peruse, for whom 'twas written,
He then will know if I am heretic.

    Bishop of London (springing from his seat).   How,
      how !   Is this tribunal then too small
For you to render answer for your sins ?
Do you not know the powers we are vested with ?
Do you not know that we do hold the power
To place you now in prison for your words ?
So when we thus accuse you, you but bring
Some lying parchment to shield off our wrath :—

> [*Imitating him.*

" This let the POPE peruse for whom 'twas written,
He then will know if I am heretic."

    Wic.   Your Grace, I·do no insult to your court.
To meet the Pope I stand before you now,
Therefore in answering I address the Pope.
As for your threat of prison—I care not.

    Bishop.   Oh, erring man ! learn to repent in time ;
A prison's walls are not so spacious
That you would find much pleasure in the same.
(*To the* ARCHBISHOP.)   My lord Archbishop, do I not say
    true ?

    Arch.   Myself I do advise the prisoner
'To give his answer here before our court.
Perhaps we shall be gracious to his cause.

Wic.   Your Grace, I thank you for your courtesy,
But now for many years ye all have heard me ;
Ye know my doctrine, having heard my words,
Therefore I add no word before you now.
Judge me as you have heard me or forbear.

   Bishop.   We have this duty sent us by the Pope.

   Arch.   Unlucky man ! learn to reflect in time,
Before we banish you to some lone prison
Until we hear what judgment comes from Rome.

   Wic.   Your Grace, I am determined.   Sentence me.

   Voices.   Room for Sir Henry Clifford in the chapel !

   Bishop.   Your Grace, it is expedient that we should.

   Voices.   Hear ye, a message from the new King's mother !

   Arch.   What noise is that ?   I hear the new King's
      name.

   Bishop.   Let Wiclif be despatched.   That can come
      later.

   Enter SIR HENRY CLIFFORD, *followed by a few* Attendants.

Clifford.   I am Sir Henry Clifford.
Bishop.   Who is he ?
   Cliff.   An officer of the Princess of Wales,
The mother to the King.   She doth command
Ye shall abstain from passing final judgment
On the accused.

   Bishop.   The judgment is pronounced !

   Cliff.   Pronounced !

   Bishop.   Or will be shortly.   He's condemned !

   Cliff.   Such shortly shall be never.   That I know.

[*Meanwhile the* Citizens *have been forcing their
way into the chapel; they surround* SIR
HENRY CLIFFORD *and his* Attendants *and*
WICLIF.

Cits. Ay! he speaks true.   He has done nothing wrong.

Bishop (excitedly). Quiet, ye rabble!   Hear the officer!

Cits. Rabble, he called us!   So, yoho, yoho!

A voice. No, we will not!   We know what he would
say,

And he is for us.   Give us Master Wiclif.

Bishop. My mind doth swim.   Oh! to touch ground at
last!

Cliff. I say again, ye shall not touch this man.

The Princess, mother of our royal King,

Doth now command it.

Arch.   It were best to yield.

Bishop. Your Grace may yield, not I.

Cits. Give us our Master Wiclif.

Cliff.   The Queen commands it.

Bishop. The Papal power is greater than the Queen.

A voice. Not greater than the People.   Give us him.

Bishop (standing up). He is our prisoner by Papal Bull.

Cliff. And I defend him here against the Pope.

Cits. We will protect him.

Voices (without).   Hail, all hail!

Freedom!   The People's liberty!   They come!

Bishop. "They come!"   Who come?

Voices (as before).   Room for the messenger!

A voice. Stand close by Master Wiclif to protect him.

Voices. Now, let him pass ! A messenger has come.
Room, room !

A Messenger *bursts through the crowd dusty and breathless.*

Messenger. Your Graces, all the land is risen !
The people are in arms in Kent and Essex,
In full revolt against the government.
A hundred thousand people march on London !

Bishop. See to your homes !

A voice.   Nay rather, see to yours !

Bishop (*whispers to the* ARCHBISHOP, *then aloud*). We
     do release the prisoner from our grasp
On this most sudden news.

Cits.   Saved, saved !

A voice.   `   Now forth,
There is no time to lose !

Another voice.   Join the revolt !

Another. Seize both the bishops !

Bishop.   Now, by Holy Mary !
Sir Henry Clifford, 1 entreat you now,
If you do reverence this kingdom's Church,
Stand by the old archbishop and myself,
And so protect us with your soldiers here.

> [*The* People *make a rush at the dais.* SIR HENRY
> CLIFFORD *brings his guard forward. They
> present their halberts against the* People.
> *They fall back.*

A voice. Delayed, but not prevented.

The cits.   Liberty !

> [*The curtain falls.*

ACT IV.

―――

THE PEASANTS' REVOLT.

―――

1381-2.

Scene I.

A room in the ARCHBISHOP'S *Palace at* Lambeth. *The* ARCH-
BISHOP OF CANTERBURY, *the* BISHOP OF LONDON, *and* WICLIF.

Archbishop.   Unholy man!   For this now raised revolt
You are responsible!

Wiclif.   How so, your Grace?

Bishop.   "How so?" you ask; like any guiltless lamb;
When all the land is filled by your exertions
With villainous monks who teach the folk to rise!

Wic.   Your Grace, you do forget that I do wear
The self-same livery of God as you.
If I do preach what Christ Himself did teach,
Is that unholy?   If I do let them know
The words of God to heal their souls therewith
And give them comfort for a little while,
Is that unholy?

Bishop.   But you have taught them
To give no maintenance to our Mother Church
Upon compulsion or as bounden duty.
If they do add to that, and so refuse
To serve beneath their masters in the realm,
But following your words to their conclusions,
Are you not guilty?

Wic. That which I do preach
Is but consistent with the former time,
When Paul did work with hands in making tents,
And other men who followed after Christ
Were simple fishers. I but preach again
The simple doctrine of my Master Christ.

    Arch. Most erring man! The devil's bonds do hold
        you.
The Lord have mercy on your erring soul!

    Wic. The Lord, your Grace, is always merciful.
He will not let me err.

    Bishop. Then we do err?

    Wic. Thou sayest.

    Bishop. Out! Away from us, bold man!
Relieve us of thy presence while thou mayest;
Later, perhaps, thou wilt not go so quick!

    Wic. I leave you, as you wish it. Soon, perhaps,
Yourselves shall *know* that I do speak the truth.

                           [He goes out.

    Bishop. What say you to this rising, good your Grace?
It doth seem dangerous.

    Arch. I cannot tell.
For it may be that it will turn to nought,
As many such.

    Bishop. I fear it is not so,
For I do hear the rebels are increasing.
Over nine counties the revolt has spread.
It will take much to stop it.

    Arch. Courage still!

A mighty storm that rages in the night
Doth leave the sky unclouded by the morn.
  Bishop.   But not before full many a tree is fallen
That sheltered many birds before the blast.

SCENE II.

Open country near London. *The camp of the* Revolters. *A distant
  view of* London *in the background.* WAT TYLER, *the leader
  of the Revolt, and others.*

  1*st Revolter.*   Speak, Master Walter, what do you
      propose ?
  Wat Tyler.   Our army is a hundred thousand men,
We are invincible !
  Revolters.   Invincible !
  Wat T.   Where all are good, this plan we find the best—
To march on London and attack the King,
Who has not stirred to meet us.   Thereupon
Will we destroy the nobles' palaces,
And open all the prisons.   We shall find
Full staunch supporters in those prison walls.
This done, we will attack the fattening sheep
Who batten on our substance in the Church.
And thereupon the whole broad land is ours,
And we ourselves will hold a Parliament
To banish from the realm our enemies.
England shall then have peace for many years.—
  Rev.   England in peace ! and justice in the land !
  Wat T.   We will have justice, e'en though many fall !
For those who fall have well deserved their fate.

It shall be just to live as other men,
Not live upon them as these men have done—
Upon our labour.   We will set them down.

> *Rev.* Down with our masters ! Comrades, hew them
>   down !

> *Wat T.* But we must stand together as one man,
And act in concert.   Then we will not stop
Till every palace in the land is burnt,
Till every noble is banished from the realm,
Till every bishop is by us beheaded,
And every county made for ever free !

> *Rev.* All England free ! and justice in the land !
Lead on, we follow—one united band !

> *Wat T.* Comrades, I thank you.   No time must be lost.
Our foes will muster if we linger long,
But now, if we do strike, they are defenceless.
Follow !   I lead you on to victory !

> *Rev.* Lead on ! We follow you to victory.
We fight for England's freedom and her right !

[They go out.

Scene III.

The same.   Some Camp Followers *still lingering.   Enter a* Messenger *hurriedly.*

> *Messenger.* Is Master Wat the Tyler on in front ?

> *A Camp Follower.* He is ; make a haste, and you will
>   overtake him.

> *Another.* What news, good fellow, have you for our
>   chief ?

Mess. News of the foe !

2nd Camp Follower.   Where are they ?

Mess.   Wholly vanished.

The baby King of fifteen sunny summers

Cannot compel his army to advance.

They say they will not fight with their own blood !

    Camp Followers. Praised be the Lady Mary ! We are
       safe.

Mess. The city is in uproar, ready to join

These forces when they near their boundaries.

Only the Mayor of London, with a few,

Have joined their part with the youthful King.

The road 'twixt here and London is all clear !

    Camp Followers. Haste on ! Our leader is before us
       on the way !

The road is clear ! Then London will be sacked !

    Mess. Spread round the news, 'twill make our courage
       rise !   [*He hurries out.*

SCENE IV.

A narrow street in London. *Two* Old Citizens *meeting*.

    1st Citizen. Gramercy ! They do say the foe has
       reached

As far as Richmond, having passed the night

At Kingston. In two hours they will be here !

O Lady Mary ! Mercy on my bones !

    2nd Cit. Courage, old friend ! They touch not such
       as us.

Had we been great, we, too, had known great sins ;

But since that we are poor, praise holy Mary !
They touch not such as us, praise holy Mary !

   1st Cit. I would that they had kept where they were
    born !

There might they march the livelong summer's day.

   2nd Cit. Well, well ! God gave us legs, so we may use
    them.

I shall not stay long by.

   1st Cit.   Nor I, please God !

Yet I do wish I knew whereto to go.

   2nd Cit. Why, come with me, and we will go together.

They will not want old men like us to fight.

                   [An alarm is sounded.

   1st Cit. Why, mercy ! They are on us, let us haste !
   2nd Cit. Why, yes. But would I know where we
    should haste to.

                         [They go out.

SCENE V.

The Gateway before the Palace of the DUKE OF LANCASTER *in the
Savoy. The* Citizens *in revolt.* Soldiers *on the walls. Enter*
WAT TYLER *surrounded by his* Guard, Peasants, *etc.*

Wat Tyler. Here are we all at last, within the city !

Revolters. England and freedom ! Justice in the land !

Wat T. Already have our friends possessed the Tower !

Now will we turn upon the nobles' houses !

Whose is this palace ?

   A Citizen.   This ? 'Tis John of Gaunt's,

The Duke of Lancaster's.

Wat T.   What!   The King's uncle's?
Down with the palace!   Comrades, to the charge!

> [*A general assault.   The* Soldiers *try to defend
> the Palace.*

Rev.   England and Liberty!   For justice now!
Soldiers.   You untrained villains!   God defend the
      right!

> [*They are beaten off, many being wounded.*

Wat T.   What! are you beaten?   Forward once again!

> [*They rush forward again.*

Rev.   England and liberty!   We fight for freedom!
Sol.   We fight for order!   God defend the right!

> [*They are again beaten off.*

Wat T.   Fire!   Fire!   Bring fire, and burn the palace
      gates!
Now will we burn them out like stinking rats!

> [*Faggots are brought and lighted torches.   The
> Revolters rush forward again.   This time the
> Soldiers give way, and retire within the Palace.
> The gates are burst open, and the Revolters
> rush through the flames up to the walls of the
> Palace,* WAT TYLER *at their head.   He rushes
> on to the drawbridge os it is being lifted, and
> cuts the cords with his sword.   It falls back.
> At the same time the portcullis falls.*

Rev.   England and freedom!   Justice in the land.
Wat T.   Delayed, but not defeated!   Bring more fire!

> [*Fire is brought and laid round the portcullis.*

Now in a few minutes will the posts be burned!

A revolter. The postern is unguarded! Seize the gate!

> [*Some* Revolters *rush out, shouting the war cry.*

Wat T. Comrades, guard here. I go to help them!

> [*He goes out. Cries from the background are heard.*

Cries. England and liberty! England and freedom!
We fight for justice! Ho! The port is gained!

> [*Smoke is seen arising at the back of the Palace.*

Rev. The palace ours! England and liberty!

> [*Some more* Revolters *rush out.* WAT TYLER *appears on the walls.*

Wat T. England and liberty! The palace is ours!

> [*The portcullis is raised. The* Revolters *rush in.*

The palace is in flames. Let none be saved!

> [*Several battlements, etc., fall.* WAT TYLER *descends and appears below.*

This is the first. It shall not be the last.
First princes, and then priests, and then the king!

> *Enter a* Messenger.

Messenger. Captain! The Archbishop is prisoner,
Being captured in the grounds of Lambeth Palace.
The company that seized him does convey him
Straight to the Tower; he will be here anon.

Wat T. When he doth reach the Tower, there shall he
    die!
For who would fall upon a vermin brood
And not destroy the mother of them all?

[In the background WICLIF crosses the stage, followed by some Mendicants with angry gestures. He is caught sight of by those in front.

Rev. (*in the foreground*).   Wiclif!   The   poor   man's
    friend!
Mendicant Monks.   But this duke's friend!
No friend to the revolt!   A heretic!
Rev.   The poor man's friend!   No harm shall come to
    him!
Stand back!

        [They draw WICLIF to the front of the stage, driving off the Mendicants.

Wat T. (*to the* Mendicants).   You fought for us!   Then
    fight not now against us!
You are of our own party.   You should know
More sure respect for those that succour us.

Enter a company of Revolters, *drawing in the* ARCHBISHOP OF CANTERBURY *on a cart, bound.* WAT TYLER *steps forward and stops them.*

One moment!   We have yet a word to say
To this your prisoner.   Simon Sudbury,—
For such alone you are without your titles,—
For your own sins are you before us now
A prisoner,—yours and the Church's sins,
Which grew together under prelacy—
And for them must you suffer as you will.
Blame not the poor, upon whose bread you live,
That they do rise and take them back again
The life which by that food was nourishèd.
Old man!   I would have spared you this last stroke,

8

But Vengeance, that doth know no dalliance,
Doth cry out for your blood, for tyrant's blood.
(*To the* Guards.)   Lead on, and straight to execution !
 Arch.   One moment bid them stay !   An old man asks !

     [WAT TYLER *signs to them to halt.   They do so.*

You, who do seem their leader, and all you
Gathered in full revolt against the King,
I turn me, erring fighters, to address you !
     In a few hours
This voice I have will be for ever silent.
(*Regarding his bonds.*)   Think not that I am conquered
   by these bonds,
For were I free I would not keep my life
Longer than I could serve my country's King.
I shall not falter to the very end.
But you, who stand around me, upon you
For this day's work the curse of God is fallen,
For taking in your wrath the innocent blood,
The Lord's anointed !   Woe ! I say to you
Who hear me now and do not yet repent !

    [*A few* Revolters *kneel at the foot of the cart.*

Woe ! I do say to you, to all of you
Who work this deed of blood within our land,
Who take a brother's not a foeman's blood.

    [*A* Revolter *draws* WAT TYLER *apart   The*
    ARCHBISHOP *stops, observing him.*

 1st Rev.   My captain !   This your sentence is severe.
I pray you, think upon it !
 Wat T.   It cannot be !

Were one forgiven, all must be forgiven.

> [*They look at the* ARCHBISHOP.

Arch.   The Church's blood is not as others' blood !
The Church's blood that flows from martyrs' veins
Is aye the Church's seed !   Think not to tame
With such misdeeds the holy spirit of men !
Think not to kill the Eternal Life of God !

> [WICLIF *approaches* WAT TYLER *and converses
> apart, but aloud.   The* ARCHBISHOP *as before.*

Wic.   Sir, or Sir Captain ! I do pray you now
To deal more mercifully with his Grace.
I and his own grey hairs do beg for him.

Wat T.   It cannot be !

Arch. (*breaking in*).   Priest Wiclif !   Not for me
Be thy prayers uttered.   On thy unholy head,
More than on any others, rests God's curse
For this rebellion,—thine, which many years
Hath preached unholy doctrine in this land,
And stirred by thy supporters every spot
That had been ever peaceful.   Thou alone
Hast more to answer for than all these here,
These sheep, who gather round thee thus astray !—
Upon his soul be merciful, great God !

Wic. (*walking forward to the foot of the cart*).   Your
        Grace ! whom still I call by his own name,
England's Archbishop—for as such you are—
Hear me for this short space, lest you should go
Into Eternity, before God's Throne,
With this untruth, this lie, upon your lips !

Never—let him accuse me who hath heard me—
These many years have I once taught to men
To do such deeds as you do charge me with.
Untouched by me, unasked, unwished, unprayed,
You go to your last suffering—if you go.
That I have preached against unrighteousness,
E'en when it touched your Grace, yourself doth know ;
That I fight with injustice all men know.
But, that I show you how myself doth live,
(*Kneeling before him*) Here do I kneel to pray God for
     your soul,
And—for a man may speak of deeds, not do them —
I pray to God to turn this captain's mind,
That he may yet retract; (*turning to* WAT TYLER) be
     merciful !

    Wat T. Mercy these have not known. He shall have
     none !

    Wic. (*to the* ARCHBISHOP). The die is cast. You can
     hope nothing further !

    Wat T. (*to the* ARCHBISHOP'S *guards*). I bade you
     once !—lead on to execution !

    Arch. Not yet, not yet ! Let not an old man's curse
Remain upon you when his heart doth bless ;
For One hath said, "Bless them that curse you, bless
And curse not,"—therefore take ye all from me
My blessing. God above be merciful
As you have shown no mercy unto me.
Within your souls let heavenly wisdom shine.
And may we all remeet in heaven at last !

[WAT TYLER *signs to the* Guards *to proceed. The*
ARCHBISHOP *is drawn off the stage.* WICLIF
and WAT TYLER *remain standing in deep
thought.*

Father, forgive them !   They know not what they do !

[*A long pause.*

A voice.   What!   All turned milksops !   Onward to
the fray !

A few.   Ay !   Onward !

A voice.   Where then next ?

Another.   Tyler, lead on !

Wat T.   Ay ! let us not linger here !   What ho ! for
freedom !

[*He seizes a banner and rushes out, followed by
the* Revolters.   WICLIF *remains standing as
before.*

Rev.   England and liberty !   We fight for justice !

[*Their cries are heard further and further away.*

England and liberty !   We fight for freedom !

[*After a long pause.*

Wic.   O God !   That I have lived to see this day !

SCENE VI.

The same as before. WICLIF *standing alone. Enter several* Mendicant Monks *conversing. On seeing* WICLIF *they stand back.*

1*st Mend.*   See where the scheming hypocrite is standing.
He seems much moved, as he indeed should be
After such action and such treachery.
The very ground on which he stands is poisoned.

2*nd. Mend.*   How like the Arch-Deceiver he doth look !

To think that such a man should so deceive us.
He cannot be, I say, the people's friend.
(*Aloud, so as to attract* WICLIF'S *attention.*)   I hate you!
                    [WICLIF *turns round and regards them.*
People's friend!   Their Arch-Deceiver!
Who preached against the evils of the land,
And who doth now again enrich himself
By making friends with those who should destroy him?
Thou artful serpent!

 Wic.   Brothers! I catch you not!
If I do ought amiss then do you tell me;
It is a friend's task, and much more a brother's.

  1st Mend.   Ay! we will tell you!   Who preached at
   the Church
At wasted revenues and ill-won means?
Who now beneath the storm doth shelter him
Under the bended oak?

 Wic.   Brothers, I do no wrong.
That I have preached against the Church's evils
You fully know.

  1st Mend.   Yourself art part of it!
What of your flock and of your pastorate?

 Wic.   I render thanks to Heaven, they are safe!

 2nd Mend.   Yet we have none!

 Wic.   All office is not one!

 2nd Mend.   You take the Church's moneys. 'Tis enough!

 Wic.   Brothers, you are too rash upon this matter!
All I have preached is on the revenues
Which are distributed so wrongfully

Among those men who do no work for it.
The labourer is worthy of his hire.

  3rd Mend.   Nay! Hear him not! He does but mock at
    us!
The servant of the Duke of Lancaster
Is not the people's friend!

  1st Mend.   (*To* WICLIF.)   Enough, old man!
We have enough of your fine sophistries.
Yet fear us still.   The poor have learnt to fight!

  2nd Mend.   The people's friend!

> [*They go out,* WICLIF *is left standing alone.*

  Wic.   So these are turned against me!   These poor men,
Who call themselves the followers of Christ!
O God! O God! that I must stand alone!
(*Thinking.*) Mine own familiar friend, in whom I trusted,
Who walked with me within the house of God,
Hath lifted up his heel against me.   O God!
Help me to bear it!   All could I have borne,—
All, but not this!   It is too much!

> [*He pauses for a long while.*

                    Yet still,
I do remember words which speak to me.
How runs it?   They do seem to leave me now.
" Put not thy trust in princes," so it reads,
" Nor any child of man."

> [*He throws himself on a stone bench.   A long pause.*

                    I must not stay!
Life calls to action, not to useless tears.

> [*As he goes out the curtain slowly falls*

Scene VII.

Wiclif's *lodging in* London. Janet *alone.* *Enter* Wiclif.

Jan. Father! What news?

Wic.   Ay! weighty news, my love!
Wat Tyler is beheaded! The revolt
Is at an end! The rebel crowds are scattered,
And every man doth flee to his own home.
The Mayor arrested him, close by, at Smithfield,
When he approached the King! 'Tis at an end!

> [*He throws himself into a chair.* Janet *totters
> towards him, and, falling at his feet, buries
> her face in his lap. After a long pause* Janet
> *raises her head and looks up into his face.*

Jan. My Father! will they leave you now alone?

Wic. It cannot be! For the Archbishop's blood
Doth weigh against me in their reckonings.
The Duke of Lancaster, the Princess Joan—
None now support me. Haply I shall fall.
Who can touch pitch and keep him undefiled?

Jan. (*as before*). Where is John Horn?

Wic.   My love, I know not yet.

> [*A long pause.*

Enter a Messenger.

Mess. I come to summon you before the Bishop,
The highest prelate left,—the Bishop of London,—
To answer to the charge of treachery
Against the King, and also heresy.
As twice before, against the Pope of Rome.
The day which is appointed is in May,
The seventeenth; and Blackfriars is the place

Arranged, within the monastery there
Of the Dominicans.   The whole great Church
Will be assembled then to meet you there.
You have my message.

 Wic.   I do thank you for it !

 Mess. And your answer ?

 Wic.   That I meet them there.

     [*The* Messenger *leaves a parchment on the table*
      and goes out. JANET *is heard weeping.*

Janet, why weep you now ?   The hour is come !
And I fear nothing.

 Jan.   Father ! comfort me.

When you are gone, I shall be left alone !

 Wic. (*quietly*). I know of one who still will comfort you.

 Jan. God is so far.

 Wic. (*as before*). I mean, love, one on earth.

       [*She looks up into his face.*

He will protect you after I am gone.

    [*She bursts out again weeping, and buries her face
     in his lap.*

      Enter JOHN HORN.

 John. I come unluckily in time it seems.

        [JANET *starts up.*

 Wic. Ah no ! Indeed you come most opportunely,
For I have work which none but you can do.
You know the troublous times which we have passed
Are over—for the many, not for me.
To-day I have received another summons
To answer for my action in the matter.

And as of old for ancient heresy.

(*To* JANET.)   My child, let me be here alone to meet it;
Go you to Lutterworth and wait my coming,
As I *will* come.   I do that I do promise.
You, pupil John, shall see her to our home;
There is much work which needs performing there.
Go, I do ask you.   It were safer there
Than here in London, where man is not safe
From changing passions and from changing rule.

Jan.   My father, I did come to comfort you.

Wic.   And comfort you have been,—I know that well,—
Sweet comfort such as old men ever love.
Let me find *that* when I do come back home.

Jan.   You do command me when you only ask:
Therefore I go, but all unwillingly.

Wic.   You do not go alone.

John.   Not all alone.

> [*Going to* JOHN HORN *laughing, but with tears
> still in her eyes.*

Jan.   Yet it were best to go with both together.
But as you wish it, father, so it is.

Wic.   I wish it, love.   Nay! ask no more of me.
John Horn, be ready with to-morrow's dawn,
There is no use in tarrying hereabouts.

John.   Master, I will.   But will you stay alone?

Wic.   Ay! all alone.   I do not fear the devil.
But hurry now, you have no time to lose.

> [JOHN HORN *takes* JANET'S *hand and kisses it,
> then goes to* WICLIF.

Be ready in the early hours with post-horses
And due provisions.   Now 'twere best to go.

  John (kneeling before WICLIF).   Your blessing, master.

  Wic.   Ay ! you have it, son !

  John (in going, aside).   Tempora mutantur, when young
    priests so
Accompany their lady loves away
To distant homes.   Ay ! but my star is lucky !

                              [*He goes out.*

  Wic.   But now, my child, seek you some slight repose ;
To-morrow with the day be up and going.

  Jan.   O father ! why remain so desolate ?

  Wic.   The spirit, not the flesh, compels me to it.
All will be bright ere long.

  Jan.   I hope so, father.

  Wic.   Then as a worthy daughter leave me now,
And sleep you sweetly.   So, good-night.

  Jan.   Good-night !

                              [*She goes out.*

  Wic.   Alone !   The dark hours gather one by one
To their completion in the fall of time.
I stand in hazard on the river's brink—
Either I reach the shore, or with the stream
Am swept away with strength too weak to last.
But once across, and then the way is clear.
Man walks by faith, but faith has need of sight,
God's giving to us men as heritage,
In compensation for the body's life,
Which is a life that lives within a corpse.

To new encounters am I called then now,
And go to meet them.   Once more have I need,
Once more I pray as oftentimes before—
God give me strength to conquer.

Scene VIII.

Interior of the Hall of the Dominican Monastery in Blackfriars.
Wiclif's *trial.   Ten Bishops, sixteen Doctors of Law, thirty
Doctors of Theology, and Four Bachelors of Laws are assembled.
The whole Hall is full of retainers, etc.* Wiclif *standing in
the midst.   The* Bishop of London *in the robes of the* Arch-
bishop of Canterbury *conducting the council.*

Bishop of London.   Wiclif, of your misdeeds the world
        is sick !
My brother's blood—his who did fill this chair—
Doth cry against thee, in a cry of vengeance.
I have no words to lavish.   Thou dost know
All I would say against thee.   If, in turn—
If you have ought to answer to our charge
Then speak ; if you have not, be silent now ;
We know your doctrines.
Wic.   Doctrines, your Grace, have I
None other than of Truth.   But, for you say—
You know them, as indeed I think you do—
I will not speak upon them.   All besides,
My life, my faith, my deeds, my everything—
You know as well.   I do not trouble you
With longer speech.   Give judgment as you will !
    Bishop.   What !   do you answer nothing to our charge ?
    Wic.   Nothing, my lord !   High-priests I answer so !

Many.   Blasphemer !

Wic.   Ye have said it !

Many.   Judgment, judgment !

Bishop. Think once again !   Yet could I wish to save you.

Wic. There is no need, my soul being wholly saved.

My lords, I am not Christ, now to command

A myriad angels for my company.

Nor am I Samson that with royal strength

I should pull down this structure on your ears.

   Ret. (in the background).   Nay ! hear him not ! hear
      not his blasphemy !

Wic. My lords !

Ret.   We will not hear him !   Heretic !

Wic. Nay, hear me !

Ret.   Hear we will not !   Judgment, judgment !

Bishop (rising from his seat).   My lords ! have patience
      for a little while.

Ret. Judgment.   We wait for judgment !

Bishop.   That shall be !

I pray you, hear this man, what he would say !

   Ret. Judgment.   We wait for judgment !

> [*At this moment an earthquake is felt throughout
> the whole Hall.   The entire assembly rise to
> their feet.   The earthquake continues some
> minutes, images falling and windows crashing
> in.   A large fresco of the* MADONNA *falls down,
> and a painting of Pope Innocent III. and
> Urban VI. fall.   The people rushing about in
> consternation.*

Wic.   Judgment comes !

> [*The curtain falls.*

ACT V.

LUTTERWORTH.

1382-4.

ACT V.

SCENE I.

The banks of the Swift *by its junction with the* Avon. *In the background on a hill the Norman Chapel of* Brownsover. JANET *is walking along the bank, picking flowers. Evening.*

Jan. How late he is! I thought that he would come
Sooner, and now the afternoon is dying
Behind the hills, and I must soon hie homewards.
I wonder how the issue fared with him
Before the court. He said that he should conquer,
And I must trust,—hard task when all alone
Fearing the contrary. How brave he is!
Ah! there's an iris,—now the flower's mine;
And there's another—that shall be mine too!
He said that he would come ere afternoon,
And yet he comes not. They have kept him back,
Perhaps in prison. Oh, those cruel men!
What should they find so fearful in his ways?
The people trust him, and the poor adore him
As their protector. Yet he does not come!
It cannot be that he forgets his promise;
And yet this was the day. Oh, England, England!
So fair a land and yet so full of woe,

9

Which he alone has faith to overcome.

No, no! I must not falter.   I'll be brave,

And *know* he's coming.   Yet the daylight dies.

That lily's mine !   Ah, I have reached it now !

[Singing.

> Swift and Avon flow together—
>> Brook and stream with mingled wave.
> I watched in every kind of weather
>> The spot where they their trysting have.
>>> Swift and Avon flow together,
>>> They are one for evermore.

> Here the stream, his first love meeting,
>> Held her faithful to the end,
> Down their course together fleeting
>> Wheresoe'er their course might wend.
>>> Swift and Avon flow together,
>>> They are one for evermore.

> Gladly 'neath the ocean standing,
>> Death is Life in the ocean's roar ;
> Swift and Avon know no parting,
>> They are one for evermore.

[A bell sounds from the chapel.

>>> Swift and Avon flow together,
>>> They are one for evermore.

Now for some ragged-robins.   Here they grow !

These are to deck his table where he sits.

He loves the wild flowers that grow hereabouts

Better than all the rest.   How sweet they are !

I wish that he would come.   How late he is !

[The bell sounds again.

Ah ! there's the bell that tolls the end of the day

And calls to vespers.   I must hurry home,

[The bell keeps tolling.

Or else the night will catch me, lingering
Before I reach there safely.   Now's the hour
I love the most in all the livelong day,
And it goes by so quickly.   One flower more—
That ox-eyed daisy!   Now I hasten home.
I wish that he would come.   'Tis very late.

[She goes out.

SCENE II.

The same.   An old Countryman *hurrying home from work, carrying his tools.   Enter a* Messenger.

Mess.   Good-evening, master !   Is this same the way
To Lutterworth ?
Countryman.   The Lady Mary bless you !
Ay ! that it is ; but you have far to go,—
Some good six miles if you keep by the path,
And the night draws in.   What do you out so late ?
Mess.   I come from Master Wiclif, to inform
The good folk of his household that he comes,
Though somewhat hindered.
Country.   Ay ! you come from him ?
Mess.   Ay ! he's my Master, that is plain enough.
Were I not here if it was otherwise.
God's love be with you.   I must hurry on.
Country.   You be from Master Wiclif !   Then you know

[Detaining him.

How went the day with him and what he said.
Did he wax eloquent ?   What's the issue on it ?
Mess.   Ay ! many things !   But he has won the day.
Howbeit by a marvel he is safe.

Country. Bless Lady Mary! Did he fear for ought?
But no! he's brave as soldiers,
And strong as lions, and, as God's Book says,
As wise as serpents and as calm as doves.
Himself did tell us when he preached up there
In the little chapel. 'Lady! it is late.

Mess. Ay! marvellous things there were; but now,
 good-even,
I loiter badly. God's love go with you.

Country. Our Lady bless you!
 [*The* Messenger *goes out.*
Ay! what times these are!
1 didn't think to lose my son in war
In his own country; yet the boy is dead.
God rest him! and his soul is now at peace.
—How all those nobles pressed us! Jesu's blood!
But now the trouble's over—God be praised!
And now comes Master Wiclif home again.
Ay! He's the man to know the will of God.
1 know it when 1 hear him. Ah! he's kind,
And loved my son, too, as though he were his own;
Though he had none to bless him; and mine's dead.
Well, well! The dead's forgotten, God have mercy!
 [*He goes out.*

SCENE III.

The same. Night. Enter WICLIF *alone.*

Wic. Six miles from home. The night is very dark,
But I should know the pathway. Here it is!
How still the night is, and the stars are out!

It is not long before the morning now,
Yet I reach home ere morn.   Oh, Avon stream,
How I do love your bank!   The waters flow
A long way on before they join the sea
Down in the west where I have never been,
But may be some day ; who can ever tell ?
And here's the Swift, that leads back to my home !
Ay ! you are dear as Avon, my own brook
That flows down from my village.   Many a time
Have I found comfort, wandering by your side,
And thinking of the great world far away,
That knew not of you.   You my comfort were
Ay ! many a time when councils raged at me.
Methinks I could be happy could I stay
Aside of you, and be a part of you—
So close together grown.   And like a flower
That grows upon your banks draws life from you
And yet adds ornament—so could I be !
Ah ! I grow childish.   I must hasten on,
Else the equipage which I left behind,
To rest the night at Dunchurch, will be there
Before me.   I must hasten quickly on.

                                   [*He goes out.*

SCENE IV.

A gallery, or passage, in WICLIF'S *house at* Lutterworth.   JANET,
      just returned, alone.   Enter a Serving Maid.

   Maid.   Mistress Janet, there's a messenger arrived
Who seeks to see you   Shall I bring him to you ?
   Jan.   Yes ! bring him to me.   He has brought me news
                                   [*The* Maid *goes out.*

Of my dear uncle.   Oh, how my heart beats!
I would I knew his message.

Enter the Messenger.

Mess.   Is this the lady
To whom my master sent me on ahead?

Jan.   Who is your master?

Mess.   Master Wiclif.

Jan.   Good.
Then bring me joyful tidings.

Mess.   That will l,
For now my master follows very soon,
And sent me on directly he arrived
At Dunchurch, to bring tidings that he came,
That all was well, and he for exercise
Would wander through the fields, and be here now
As soon as might be.

Jan.   Say, how went the day?

Mess.   Most marvellously.   An earthquake was felt,
Such as hath ne'er been known in memory
Of living man.   The bishops were dismayed,
And broke the trial off without delay.
It is in judgment, so do many say,
For handling our dear master as they did.

Jan.   l know enough, and thank you.   Leave me now.
The servants will provide you for your wants.
I thank you.   Leave me.   l have need of rest.

[*The* Messenger *goes out.   She sounds u bell.*
Enter Serving Maid.

Esther, place a light in my uncle's study,

For I shall watch for him.

Maid.   You are tired, Mistress Janet.

Jan.   Yet will I watch.   Go do as I have bid you.

> [*As the* Maid *goes out the curtain falls.*

SCENE V.

WICLIF'S *study at* Lutterworth.   *At the back a large window with
   balcony steps that lead down into the garden.   The window open.
   Night.* JANET *alone.*

Jan.   So long the hours are, yet he does not come !

The messenger was certain he would follow

Not far behind, and now 'tis almost morn.

How tired I am !   Yet he'll be glad to see me

When he gets back to home.   What he has suffered !

I know not whether I should all believe

The marvels that the messenger related.

Such things have been, but yet not here in England.

And yet, perhaps,—who knows ?   Perhaps it was

A judgment sent by God on those that judged him !

Yet I am glad he's safe and almost home ;

How late he is !   The church clock striking two.

> [*The church clock strikes.*

I wonder that he fears not so to go

Alone across the country ; yet he knows

The people love him like a father all,

And they would die for him as they did die,

As they believed, to serve him.   Oh, these wars !

When will they cease, and Christ reign on in peace ?

How he did suffer in those fearful days,

Longing for peace !   And yet the nobles held him

For all that carnage half responsible.

Yes! he, the man of peace and servant of Christ!

> [*She goes to the window. A bright star is visible through the top of the open window. She listens.*

The night is still, the stars begin to wane.

Ah! there's the morning star! Ah! that's my star!

A herald placed as surety for the morn.

So now the morn is near.

Was that his step?

Ah no! Only the water in the hurrying brook.

Ah me! how tired I am! Yet, when he comes,

I'll not be sleeping. He shall find me here.

His step again? Ah no! The silence mocks me.

Ah, morning star!

You watch for day and I watch for his coming.

Perhaps they'll come together, and perhaps

He'll be like you, and come before the day,

And not like you, and die away before it.

For he shall stay now with us all his days.

And yet you die not either, do you, star?

So are you like him.

> [*She leaves the window, and comes to the front of the stage with her back turned to the window, manifesting signs of fatigue. Pause.* WIC-LIF *appears up the steps of the balcony, remaining, while ascending them, a short while without, looking in. The morning star is seen shining directly over his head.*

Wic. (*seeing* JANET). Janet!

> [*He advances into the study. She rushes towards him and sinks into his arms.*

Jan.   Ah! home at last!

> [*He carries her to a chair, and sits down still hold-*
>   *ing her.*

Wic.   Yes! Home, my child.

Thank God 'tis over!

Jan   Oh, my father!

Wic.   Love,

You must be wearied. Let us seek rest awhile.

Jan.   Oh, father, 1 have watched the livelong day

And night for your home-coming. You are safe?

Wic. Yes, safe, my child! God had good care of me;

And now I come back home to you at last.

> [*The curtain falls.*

SCENE VI.

Wiclif's study as before. Morning. Wiclif alone. It is winter-time. A winter-rose is lying on the table by which Wiclif is seated.

Wic. The time wears on. It seems to me at last

That soon it will be time for me to die.

After so many tossings in the storm

The haven surely is not far from sight;

Ay! it seems close upon me. One thing more

1 ask, and one thing only, O my God!

To live in quietude among my folk,

To tender those when they have need of help,

And still do something for the mighty cause

Of England's freedom, England's liberty,

Who have done something though, God knows, how little!

(*Regarding the flower on the table.*) Ah! this is Janet's

     work! I know that well,

Who loves to make my study light and joyous
With memories of Nature such as these.

[*He takes it in his hand.*

Yes! there's philosophy in your sweet life,—
To live in silence where thou hast been planted,
And beautify the spot.   All life were good
Were we, weak men, contented so to live,
To climb up to the light which is above us,
And make our lives as beautiful as thou,
Casting a silent fragrance all around,
That men might say, " Here grows a perfect flower ! "
That were a saintly life.   But we must strive,
Being men, not flowers that perish in a day,—
Being men, not creatures merely beautiful,
With but a silent voice of ecstasy.
Ours is another labour being men,
To right the wrong and make the lie to cease,
To join in fight that peace may come at last,
To labour and to labour and to die.
Yea ! and indeed that, too, is beautiful :
A beauty of the living, not the dead,
A beauty of the spirit, not the form,
An influence that savours of the soul.
Yea ! and indeed to live is beautiful.
To live and labour is the gift of God.—
Again the pain !   Oh, give me strength awhile
To carry further what is but begun ;
It cannot be for long that I can last,
Who feel Life's winter numbing all my limbs

Like winter's snow the water into ice.
'Twill not be long, the pain which is the last,
Nor will it be so wholly sad to go
To God and to the Saviour, and the rest ;
Yet had I wished a little more of life,
A little longer still to ply the oar,
To carry still yet further on her way
The ship we sail by.   We shall sleep at last
Beneath the ████████ when our work is done,
And go unconsciously to our longed haven.

A Servant *enters.*

Where is my niece ?   I wish to see her now.

Ser. I saw her standing in the dining-hall
By the great fire, and Master Horn with her
Conversing.

Wic.   Say to them I need them both.
I wait for them within my study here.

[*The* Servant *goes out.*

Always together !   O my loving niece !
How love, the poet's weed, doth yet spring up
E'en in a young priest's heart !

[*He pauses.   Then enter*] JANET *and* JOHN HORN.
She goes up to WICLIF.

Jan.   You called us, uncle ?

Wic.   Uncle—no longer father !—eh, my child ?
You must have other thoughts within your head
Thus to forget what you had always called me.
(*Inquiringly.*) What were you thinking of ?

Jan.   Of many things.

Wic.　And you, friend John ?

John.　　　　　　　　　　　　Of many things as well.

Wic.　The same things, think you ?

John.　　　　　　　　　　　　That I cannot say.

Wic. (*stroking* JANET'S *hair*).　Nor you, my child, as
　　well.　Is that not so?

Oh, children, children !　Is an old man blind

That you do think that he can never see

What you think of each other ?　Is it ~~strange~~

If those who know the world can read your wish,

Though you have ne'er expressed it.　Janet, child !

I do not think my days can now be many

Before I journey hence.

Jan.　　　　　　　　　　Hence, father, why ?

Wic. That One does know, not I.　I do but feel

The winter's coming.

Jan.　　　　　　　　You are ill, my father ?

Wic.　Ill, my darling, no !　But night may come,

So work I by to-day.

(*Turning to* JANET *and* JOHN HORN *alternately*.)　You
　　love each other ?

Yes, I have seen it, and I see it now ;

For love knows no concealing and no bars.

That this is so I half rejoice, half grieve.

Now hear me while I speak of this to you.

You speak of love, such as all lovers know.

You know what love is ?　Let me tell it you.

It is not of the body nor the soul,

It is not of the heart nor yet the mind,

Desire, nor interest, ambition, prudence ;
But all of these together mixed, in one
Combining, like the rays which make the light.
He cannot live alone, an eremite ;
But is companionable, a comforter
That makes us ever better than we were
Before his coming,—then together go
The lifelong journey to the journey's end,
Jolting awhile across the jagged stones,
Lagging awhile among the shady hills,
O'er plain, o'er mountain, rivulet, or sea,
A summer's day or half a hundred years.
Love knows his dangers but can conquer them,
And knows his friends and those that pass as such.
Then at the last, the weirdsome journey done,
He takes us in his arms a moment's length,
And we are fanned to sleep for evermore.
Such thing is love, the love of which you speak.
But now, beware what you do christen so.
I know of many which did seem so born,
But which proved bastards ere the naming day.
(*Taking their hands.*)   Janet, can you speak thus ? and
	you, too, thus ?
Then do you know what love is, as you should.
But now—for we are stationed in a world
Where wrong is right, and right is nicknamed wrong—
There is a sorry sequel to the song.
We are of time, not of eternity ;
And English-born, not under southern skies,

In ancient times when love was callèd love.
And you and I, my son, are dubbed as priests,
As priests of Christ living in Christendom,
Which has its laws and ancient ordinance.
This to obey we are in duty bound,
Even though unjustly ordered from of old.
Yea! we are priests, and so must not know love
As Adam knew it ere he sometime fell,
As the Apostles who did follow Christ
And many others knew it. We must wait
Till time shall roll this stumbling-block away,
When you and I are mouldering in the grave,
And all the world doth wear another face.
Janet, why weep you? Man was born for sorrow.
Who knows no sorrow nor can bear his sorrow
Were best unborn. O love, O love long past,
That never more shall come again to me,
Look on me now, and with thy spirit's breath
Breathe one soft kiss upon my parchèd lips,
And let me know that thou art with me yet.

                                        [*He weeps.*

Children, if you know love, then flee from him,
But not from one another. Many a soul,
To love denied, hath found some rest at last
In labouring ever by his loved one's side—
Such life I give you. Go, loves, go and work
Within Christ's vineyard ; lo! the grapes are ripe.

                              [*A voice is heard calling.*

   Voice. Wiclif! ho, Master Wiclif! answer me!

[JOHN HORN *goes to the door of the study.*

John.   What would you ?   He, our master, is with us !

Voice.   I come to bring you news of what's a-foot.

John.   What is it ?

Voice.   Why, it seems, some mendicants—
Monks as they call them—are assembled here
To stay the master from his saying Mass,
Declaring that he is unworthy of the post,
And bringing thus their feud to our own church.

John.   Is it so indeed ?

Voice.   'Tis so, with no denying.

John.   We will see to it.   [*He closes the door.*

                    Master, did you hear ?

Wic.   I did.   They cannot now prevent me long.

John.   Will you prevent them ?

Wic.   No, Another shall.

John.   O master ! will you meet them ?

Wic.   I shall go.
My children, let me kiss you while I may.
It may not be that I shall soon be able.

Jan.   O father !

John.   Master, say not so.

Wic.   I do.
I feel my end is near.   Draw near, my children.
In after times, when I am in the grave,
You will not all forget me ; will you, love ?
But think upon the old man, how he lived,
And what he preached, and how at last he died.
You will, love, will you not ?   [*He kisses her.*

Jan. (*falling at his knees*).   Father, I will !

Wic.   For you, my son, another task remains.
You know my life and all that I have done,
And why I did it.   Follow where I led.
Before God's throne again our souls shall meet.

John (*falling at his knees*).   O father, father !

> [WICLIF *kisses him.   A long pause.   A Mass bell
> is heard, which continues ringing until the
> middle of the next scene.   A long pause.*

Wic.   Come, my children, come !

> [*He takes them by the hand and raises them.   They
> go out.   The curtain falls.*

SCENE VII.

Interior of the Church at Lutterworth.   *Many* People *assembling
for Mass.   A knot of* Mendicant Monks *standing in the Chancel.
The bell ringing.   The organ is heard playing softly.*

1*st Mendicant.*   He has been told.   He will not come
  to-day,
The coward !

2*nd Mendicant.*   Ay ! he will.

1*st Mend.*   Then let him come.
The hour draws nigh ; he should be earlier here.

3*rd Mend.*   How will you stay him ?

1*st Mend.*   That shall all men see.

2*nd Mend.*   Let it be done with order.

1*st Mend.*   Order, say you,
When he it is breaks order every day
Performing here his holy offices,
With mind fulfilled of poisonous heresies,
And thus cajoling all these poor folk's minds,

Who think that he alone can speak the truth ?
Speak not to me of any order now
When he it is breaks order and not I !

3rd Mend.   Will they not set on us, these people here,
When they perceive their pastor handled so,
And thus prevented of his offices ?

1st Mend.   Trust that to me, and never dream of fear ;
The people here, I know, are tame enough,
Else would they not endure him.

2nd Mend.   Ay ! that's so.

3rd Mend.   Then let us stand together where we are,
And wait his coming.

2nd Mend.   Hark ! the bell has stopped.

1st Mend.   Then is he coming. Now then stand together.

> [*The doors of the* Church *open, and a procession of*
> Monks *enter with candles, incense, etc.; behind*
> *them* WICLIF, JANET, JOHN HORN, PURVEY, *etc.*

Monks.   " Lucis largitor splendide,
               Cuius sereno lumine
               Post lapsa noctis tempora
               Dies refusus panditur :

               " Tu verus mundi lucifer,
               Non is qui parvi sideris,
               Venturæ lucis nuntius,
               Augusto fulget lumine.

               " Sed toto sole clarior
               Lux ipse totus et dies,
               Interna nostri pectoris
               Inluminans præcordia."

> [*In the meantime the procession has reached the*
> *Chancel.* WICLIF *passes through to the high*
> *altar.   As he passes the* Mendicant Monks,
> *the* 1st *stands out in his path. The music stops*

10

1st Mend. Blasphemer!

Wic. Brother, neither time nor place
Is this for such discussion and such charges.
I do my office. Do not hinder me.

1st Mend. 'Tis therefore that I stand here in your way,
Lest you should take the name of God in vain—
As you have done too often—once again.

Wic. I bid you once again to stand aside,
And not make brawling in God's Holy Place.

1st Mend. I bid you not defile it.

Wic. If I did,
I would not enter here.

2nd Mend. (*rushing out*). Ay! and you shall not!
Let those perform God's holy offices
Who know His word, and would not make it common
And falsified withal. The people's shepherd!
Say rather, their deceiver!

> [*Some more* Mendicant Monks *stand forward.*

Mend. Heretic!
Advance no further.

Wic. In God's sight I stand,
As well as man's. He will not let me err,
Nor will He fail me in the hour of need.
I go to do my office now. Stand back!

> [WICLIF *makes an attempt to force his way through
> them. They thrust him back. The* People
> *gradually enter the Chancel and surround the
> group.*

Mend. We will not let you pass. Beware of force!

Wic. Force cannot touch me, you unholy men!

Have you not heard, if so you have not read,
That men can hurt the body not the soul?
If you had seen the light by which I live,
If you had only known the love of God,
You would not now be here as my preventers,
But as companions in my holy work.
Is this your work, who serve the people's needs,
To come and to prevent in their own church
Those who have been appointed to perform
God's service there?
Is this your work, who should help raise the people
From ignorance to virtue, thus to make
A mockery of God before them all?
Such charges as ye bring myself will meet
Where'er you will and whensoe'er you will.
But now stand back. I go in God's own name
To do His service. Servants of God, give room!

Mend. We will not. One more strong than us must come
Before we move us from our sacred task
To stay the infidel.

Wic.   In God's own name,
Whom we do all revere, I say, stand back!

> [*He again tries to force his way through them,*
> *but they thrust him back with violence. At*
> *this the* People *rush forward.*

The People. One more strong has come! Yield place,
   you curs!

> [*The* Mendicant Friars, *seeing themselves overcome,*
> *gather quickly around their leader, the* 1st
> Mendicant.

1st Mend.   We are your friends, not foes.   He is your
foe.

> [*Pointing at* WICLIF.

The People.   He is our pastor.   What, then, do ye
here ?

A voice.   " Whoso entereth not by the right door
Into the sheepfold, but doth clamber up
Some other way, the same is a thief and robber."

The Mend.   We know God's Word as you.

The People.   Ay, then !   Stand back !

> [*The* People *thrust them back.* WICLIF *passes
> through to the high altar, the music recom-
> mencing.*

Monks.   " Adesto rerum conditor,
>   Paternæ lucis gloria,
>   Cuius admota gratia
>   Nostra patescunt corpora.

> " Tuoque plena spiritu
>   Secum deum gestantia
>   Ne rapientis perfidi
>   Diris patescant fraudibus

> " Ut inter actus sæculi,
>   Vitæ quos usus exigit,
>   Omni carentes crimine
>   Tuis vivamus legibus."

> [*As the last strophe finishes the* 1st Mendicant
> *breaks from the peasants who were holding him
> back, and, rushing up the steps of the altar,
> draws a dagger which was concealed in his
> dress.   He raises his hand to strike* WICLIF.

1st. Mend. This thing shall never be ! Blasphemer, die !
Rather than celebrate God's holy Mass
With impious hands, die thou, the heretic !

> [*The* People *rush forward and stay his uplifted*
> *arm.　The dagger falls to the ground.　They*
> *then hurl him down the altar steps, where he*
> *is pinioned by them and bound.*

The People.　Damned man !
What !　Wouldst thou stay the Lord's Anointed here ?

> [*They set on the rest of the* Mendicant Friars.

1st Mend.　Nay, spare ye them, for they are innocent
Of my design.

> [WICLIF *through all the scene standing unmoved.*

Wic.　Ay ! spare ye them indeed.
(*To 1st Mend.*) I had not thought you would have wished
　　my blood,
Being old.
The People.　What would you, master, we should do
With him who tried to kill our master here ?
Wic.　Release him.　One hath said, ye shall forgive.
The People.　So do we now release him—not forgive
　　him.

> [*They untie the bonds of the* 1st Mendicant, *and*
> *thrust him into the middle of the chancel.　He*
> *cowers down, grovelling on the ground.*

Wic. (*with weaker voice*).　Good people, who have
　　served me through long years,
And now on this last day preserved my breath,
I thank you as one thanks who has been saved
From perjured steel and murderous intent.
But, for I stand as Christ's vicegerent here,
And He hath bid us to forgive all sins

As we would be forgiven, so do you
Forgive this wretched man beneath us here.
Do you go with me ?

> [*He pauses.   They are silent.*

You are silent all ;
Then do I take my thoughts to be for yours,
And so forgive him.
(*To the* Man.)   Wretched man, arise.

> *1st Mend.*   I will not, till the days gone by be seven.
This do I self-impose for penitence.

> *Wic.*   God help thy penitence !
(*To the* People.)   But, for I feel
An awful shadow has passed over me,
And I am weak to death, I bid you now
Forbear this service in the shortest way
Which may be.   For I feel me weak to death.

> [*He lays his hand on the Monstrance.*

Thus with my hand upon the sacred Host,
Which Christ ordained for His memorial,
That we might think of Him when He was dead—
Thus do I stand before you, in your midst,
As I would be.   I feel me weak to death.

> [*Elevating towards the* People.

And thus I show you His memorial
Of His own death and precious suffering,
Who sacrificed His body for our souls.
I show you not My body in this bread,
But only, said He, as a token here
IN MEMORY I GAVE MY LIFE FOR YOU.

[*As he is holding it up before the* People *he is
struck with paralysis, and falls fainting to the
ground.   The* MONSTRANCE, *dashed from his
hands, falls on to the altar steps and breaks into
numerous pieces.*

The People.   O God! see to him!   See, the master's
fallen!

The Monstrance broken!   Help us!   God forgive!

[*The* People *and* Monks *rush forward and raise
him.   Others regard with horror the broken
vessel.*

Ah! he has fainted!   Quickly, send for help!

John Horn.   He is past help!   See, he is paralysed!

The People.   His eyes reopen!   Master, speak to us!

[*They place him in a chair.   He is silent.*

Ah God! he cannot speak!   Speak, speak to us!

Ah God! the master's dumb!

John.   Good people here,

The master's limbs are paralysed like lead,

And he hath lost the power of speech awhile.

He must be taken hence.   Ho! clear a way!

[*The* People *respectfully fall back.* WICLIF, *in the
chair, is lifted up by the* Monks.   *As they are
about to start,* WICLIF *makes a sign to the
choir.*

The People.   See, see!   He signs!

John.   Ah!   he would have them chant.

Let then a hymn be raised.

The People.   Oh, luckless day!

[*As* WICLIF *is borne down through the church the*
Monks *recommence singing.*

Monks.   " Tua nunc sancta dextera
            Tuere nos per sæcula,
            Post huius vitæ terminum
            Vitam perennem tribue.

            " Probrosas mentis castitas
            Carnis vincat libidines,
            Sanctumque puri corporis
            Delubrum servet spiritus. "

            [*While this verse is sung* JOHN HORN, JANET, *and
            the* Doctor *speak as below.*

John.   He cannot last ; alas ! he is too weak.

Jan. (rushing forward).   My father, O my father, O
    my father !

            [*She seizes hold of his hand. The* Monks *who are
            carrying the chair stop.*

John.   Janet ! this is no place for tears, sweet love.

Jan.   My father, O my father !

A Doctor (examining WICLIF*).*   Ne'er again
Shall he, thou call'st thy father, speak to thee.
His tongue, that was so golden, now is stayed
For evermore until th' eternal sleep,
To which he now will wander very soon.

Monks.   " Hæc sunt precantis animæ,
            Hæc sunt votiva munera,
            Ut matutina nobis sit
            Lux in noctis custodiam."

John.   O God ! Like this to live, like this to die !

            [*The* Monks *who are carrying* WICLIF *raise the
            chair again and move on. As they go out the
            curtain falls.*

SCENE VIII.

A corridor in WICLIF'S *house. A young* Peasant *meeting* JOHN
HORN. *It is night.*

Peasant.   How is it with our Master?

John.   He is gone!
No troubles now can touch that spirit more!

Peasant.   O Master, master!

John.   Nevermore again
Shall we behold him who our light had been.
The silver voice is silent now for ever,
And his strong spirit fled for evermore.
Let us not mourn, young man, that he is gone.
His work was finished; ours does now begin.
Upon our shoulders now the mantle falls,
And we must learn to bear it worthily,
For he hath left us much that we must do.

>   [*He passes his hand across his forehead.*

Oh! I am weary with our three nights' vigil,
And I have need of air.   Come, go with me
Into the open.   Let us breathe awhile,
Ere I return to see to those within.

>   [*They go out.*

His was a glorious and a noble life!

>   [*The scene changes.*

Scene IX.

A landscape in the Midland Counties *in winter time just before
dawn. A bright star shining in the sky.* John Horn *and the*
Peasant *are standing at the side of the stage. Voices are heard
singing.*

O Morning Star ! too bright to last till day.
O Morning Star ! too soon to fade away,
" Past is the Night," we hear your star-beams say.

O Morning Star, that diest with the light !
O Morning Star, shine on till day be bright !
It is not day, but still, ''past is the Night."

O Morning Star, borne on the morning blast,
O Morning Star, all things must die at last,
But thou shalt die not.   Lo ! " the Night is past."

[*The curtain falls.*

FINIS.

NOTES.

ONCE again the path's the same one—
  You, Jack, by my side to-day—
Seven summers since we came on,
  I and—but you've read the play.

This the very gate I spoke of—
  You remember—and down there
Rises up the church and smoke of
  Lutterworth,—you see it clear?

He seems with us as we wait here ;—
  Does it seem the same to you,
As we linger by the gate here,
  Just a moment for the view?

(Often you and I went trudging
  Through the pits for fossil rare
In our playtime, never budging
  For the weather, stare or wear.)

Do you know those glorious quarries—
  Tier on tier of sea-built lime,
Where you trace the old-world stories
  Back through pre-historic time?

There's the bluest of blue water
  That you hereabout may see—
Might have been a Larian daughter
  Strayed away from Italy.

(One day o'er the water's edges,
  Leaning, helped by some big stone,
Fumbling in among the sedges,
  Out you fetched a Saurian bone,

Best I'd known then, and you brought it,
  Washed and cleansed it from the clay;
Oh! a jewel's worth I thought it.
  So you gave it me that day.

Well, when you and I went pacing
  To this village years ago,
Just to take the needed tracing
  Of a brass there—even so,

LEANING O'ER THE BLUE ETERNAL
  WATERS, FROM THE CLAY OF TIME
PLUCKED YOU FORTH THIS GIFT FRATERNAL
  THAT I SET TO-DAY IN RHYME.

—Not the play. No! I have made it,
  Not one thought of it you knew;
But for your sake I essayed it,
  And to-day I give it you.)

And the fossil? 'Tis the friending   ˄ 月
  Of that great brave heart of his,
Which he gave me to the ending
  Of his life. Yes! here it is.

RUGBY, *December* 20, 1886.

ENVOI.

Go forth, my book, my mute companion thou
  Through silent hours e'er dreamless sleep was won—
Mute and yet speaking ever ; now
  Others shall hear thee when my task is done.

I heard thy words, which none but I could hear,
  And wrote them down upon the unstained leaf,—
When nights were long in my last sorrow-year,
  When none stood by nor any knew my grief.

Farewell, my book ! Across the wide world wander ;
  Perhaps in some few hearts thou shalt find rest ;
Others, perchance, that on thy pages ponder,
  Shall learn to fight the battle that is best.